ALSO BY PADGETT POWELL

A Woman Named Drown
Typical
Edisto Revisited
Aliens of Affection
Mrs. Hollingsworth's Men

�֍ / E D I S T O

EDI

PADGETT

STO

POWELL

Farrar, Straus and Giroux   New York

Farrar, Straus and Giroux
18 West 18th Street, New York 10011

Distributed in Canada by Douglas & McIntyre Ltd.
Printed in the United States of America
Published in 1984 by Farrar, Straus and Giroux
This paperback edition, 2009

Portions of this novel appeared in *The New Yorker*.

Library of Congress Control Number: 2008934379
Paperback ISBN-13: 978-0-374-53168-3
Paperback ISBN-10: 0-374-53168-4

Designed by Cynthia Krupat

www.fsgbooks.com

1 3 5 7 9 10 8 6 4 2

*Edisto is an area of the South Carolinian coast. Some places
in this novel are fictional. Those that are real do not
necessarily correspond to geography.*

For my family

❦ / EDISTO

The Assignment

❧ / I'm in Bluffton on a truancy spree, cutting, we call it, but all you do is walk off the unfenced yard during recess, where three hundred hunched-over kids are shooting marbles. I can't shoot a marble with a slingshot, so I split and go into Dresser's Rexall for a Coke or something, expressly forbidden me by the Doctor because it makes me hyper, she says, but should I drink milk all my life instead or go on now to house bourbon? That is not the point.

Suddenly there she is on a counter stool between me and a cherry Coke, or I'm even considering a suicide—sixteen godoxious syrups in a thimble of soda—but I can handle this disappointment. I could go to the Texaco and have a bottle and talk to Vergil. They even have Tom's peanuts for a goober-bottle rig—you just pour in the peanuts and drink. But Clyde, his pumpman, will try to take off his wooden leg on me. One day I got curious and he unbuttoned his shirt and showed me the network of sweaty straps all over his chest that holds the leg on, and

I got closer, and he loosened the straps and took down his overalls, and all of a sudden the leg was off, a small cypress log, and he bounced his stump around on the chair, pecan-colored and hard-looking, and I about fainted. Now I have to beg him to leave it on. When I get pale, Vergil will stop him. "Keep your leg on, Clyde." "Okeydoke," Clyde says, but he still fidgets with the straps and giggles.

But I don't get out of the Rexall unnoticed. She calls me over and introduces me to this gray-headed gent she's with. Now this is what gets me. She says to him, who turns out to be a barrister working land in Hilton Head, she says, "I want you to meet my protégé."

She never includes the detail I'm her son, so I put my name into the dialogue so she might have to mention the relationship. "Simons Everson Manigault," I say to him, stepping up and pumping him a three-pump country shake, squeezing harder than even the old man said to. You say it "Simmons." I'm a rare one-*m* Simons.

So she hatches a "protégé" on the guy and I think I see his face hitch to the floor a hint, as if he had a doubt about her—remarkable, this, because the lawyers I have seen, including my old man, have had better control of facial expression than any actor in the land, and I figure either something twitched him or he doesn't work on his feet. The Doctor has a bit of a reputation, you know, and a suitor outside the college where she teaches can be right skittish. The Negroes call her the Duchess. Anyway, next I look at them he is looking at her legs folded up under her on the chrome swivel stool, bulges of calf flesh pressed out firm as pull candy, so I just drift out of Dresser's—no suicide, but at least not recognized as skipping school either.

Truancy is no big deal to the Doctor anyway, because it's the "material" has her send me to public school, podunkus Bluffton Elementary, when the old man would send me to Cooper Boyd, college-prep academy for all future white doctors, lawyers, and architects in the low country. But the old man cut out some time ago. He gave me a Jack London book and coached me into the best eight-year-old short-stop in the history of the world before the book shit hit. "That kid's supposed to *read* all that?" he said. "I thought that was *your* library." He was shocked by the Plan: the bassinet bound by books, which I virtually came home from the hospital to sleep in the lee of, my toys. Like some kids swat mobiles, I was to thumb pages. Some get to goo-goo, I had to read.

It was something. He (the Progenitor) had actually built the shelves that held the Doctor's training tools, which took me straight away from our after-work grounder clinic and his idea of things. They got in it over this, one charged with sissifying and the other with brutalizing.

I suppose I became my momma's boy, at least she was still *there*, and in fact all this scribbling is directly related to her training program. It's an assignment. I'm supposed to write. I'm supposed to get good at it.

So the day I'm talking about, after leaving the Rexall, I got out of Vergil's without Clyde making me sick, got on the school bus, as usual, and fell out of it racing down the road, as not usual. I looked up from my surprise at not being dead and saw a white face, calm as an ambulance driver, among a whole gawking throng of Negroes. And reading the Doctor's toys for boys is what got me in the predicament.

That's what being a "material" hound will get you: little you who should be up in the front with the nice kids but are in the back listening to Gullah and watching, say, an eight-year-old smoke marijuana like a man in a cell block, eyes squinting toward the driver with each hissing intake of what his grandfather called hemp and took for granted, you trying to orate on the menace of the invading Arabs— "They don't ride camels and carry scimitars, but they are coming all the same; they've bought ten islands, we'll all be camel tenders soon"—when the emergency door flies open and it is not the Negroes nearest who go out and do cartwheels after the bus, it is you who gets sucked out into a fancy bit of tumbling on the macadam, spidering and rolling up the gentle massive cradling roots of an oak tree that has probably stopped many more cars with much less compassion. My tree just said *whoa.* You must see the miraculous thing it is to have avoided death by a perfect execution of cartwheels, rolling over a two-lane highway and partway *up* a tree, to clump down then with only two cracked ribs and no more for medicine than Empirin. The codeine kind not the old-lady kind. I jumped up to tell them I was not dead: Negroes from nowhere, peering at my sleeping little face framed by roots. As I looked at them, before jumping up and losing my breath to the ribs, I saw that one calm light face among them.

Anyway, that's what sniffing out things will do for you, and I was changed by discovering how close the end can be when you don't even think about your being alive, not at twelve, and that same night the one calm face among my coterie of gawkers stepped onto the porch like the process server he was, but with no papers to serve, and I felt the porch sag.

When the ambulance does get there, the Negroes tell the driver, "That the Duchess boy." So he takes me, not that I'm hurt or anything—though I am, sort of, because it hurts when I try to breathe—he takes me to Dr. Carlton back in Bluffton instead of the clinic in Beaufort, and Carlton gives me a ride home. My maternal Doctor has not missed me and has the evening set up.

It gets dark so very gradually it seems pure dark will never descend and I get moody in my new, good-as-dead outlook, walk around the place trying to savor the sudden news that I don't have to be alive, even, and turn on a few lamps. The Doctor clears up the dinner problem by assigning me left-overs, fine with me, and gets a drink and takes up on the wicker sofa, sitting on her folded legs, and drinks her drink.

These are the times that are best: when she is distracted and I am left to whatever I can manage on my own, basically provided for but maybe burn-ing meat loaf or something without a peep from her. These are times when we are least protégé and master. I can feel each drink she pours, each necessary bite of the sour bourbon on her mouth, feel it in a neutral way without any kind of judgment, I am aware is all, by the sounds of glass and wicker, of her evening and she must be as aware that I am going to bed without reading any assignments, just listening to the palmetto and waves and going to sleep.

We are well into that kind of dance this evening when Taurus shows up. Elbows on the drain counter, I am keeping my weight off my ribs and watching the food cook when I see him. You do not know what in hell may be out here on a hoodoo coast and I do not make a move. What follows is not nearly so ominous as I would sound. He don't ax-murder us or anything like that. Yet there is something arresting about this dude the moment you see him. He is shimmery as an islander's god and solid as a butcher. I consider him to be the thing that the Negroes are afraid of when they paint the doors and windows of their shacks purple or yellow. His head is cocked, his hand on the washtub of the Doctor's old wringer, its old manila rolling pins swung out to the side. When he comes up to the screen, I know I have seen his face before.

That's the assignment. To tell what has been going on since this fellow came trying to serve a subpoena to we think Athenia's daughter and scared Theenie so bad it about blued her hair. Before he came I spent most of my time at the Baby Grand— Marvin's R.O. Sweet Shop and Baby Grand, where I am a celebrity because I'm white, not even teenage yet, and possess the partial aura of the Duchess ("The Duchess boy heah!"). And I look like I hold my liquor ("Ain't he somp'm."). The trick there is to accept a new can when anybody offers and let your old one get drunk by somebody else.

And besides playing the freak I can jive a little, too, like the Arab alarum I like to ring. "If it wasn't for the *Marines* down the road, these Arabs'd do more than *buy* this place!" "Shih! Boy *crazy!*" And the dudes there play a tune back, a constant message: Life is a time when you get pleasure until somebody get your ass. And one of the ways to prolong pleasure is to not chop up time with syllables. They go for something larger than words, but no essays. This way nothing large is inaccurate, presumptuous. "Bitch look heavy." "Tell *me*." Like these James Brown guitar riffs of five notes that run twenty minutes, and then *one* of the five notes goes sharp and a statement is made. A whole evening hums, and then there's a new note—razor out. I still hit the Grand, but less now with Taurus and me doing things.

That night when he stepped on the porch and I was trying to breathe, the Doctor came to the door and stopped short of pushing it open as she would have for an ordinary visitor—he had his hand inside the rim of the wringer tub and his head was slightly cocked off at it as if he were listening to a large conch shell. I noticed then a stack of linen folded— not folded anymore, thrown—by the sink. Some kind of nut is on the porch and I take time out to notice this because now I know something is up.

Because when your Southern barony is reduced as ours is to a tract of clay roads cut in a feathery herbaceous jungle of deerfly for stock and scrub oak for crop, and the great house is a model beach house resembling a pagoda, and the planter's wife is abandoned by the planter, as ours has been, and she has only one servant left (Theenie, who for quarters has only one 10′ x 12′ shack insulated by newspaper and flour on a cold Atlantic bluff), well, that vestigial baroness insists that vestigial slave do her one duty right—"the linen," all that remains of cotton finery. Theenie vacuums the house too, but that doesn't signify as Preserving the South. And the laundry was not in the hall closet (successor to armoire) but flung all over the kitchen counter, which was not right.

If I had not rolled sixty feet at forty miles an hour into an oak tree just hours before, I might have thought nothing of that laundry. But there it was, flopped forlorn on the drainboard, looking a bit like I might have before I stood up to disassociate myself from the dead in that sudden ring of gawkers. There was somehow a connection in all this: my suddenly seeing the linen in the new good-as-dead way of seeing, the linen an embodiment of Theenie and the Doctor's old order and of, somehow, the someone cocking an ear to a sound on our porch, whose discovery stopped the Doctor mid-track and knocked her into her classroom style, so that she suddenly stood three feet inside the door, straightened up, and spoke as if there were an invisible podium between her and her audience.

"Won't you please come in and let us talk," said the Doctor heavily, as though scanning the line for a student, and she stepped forward and slowly swung open the screen door to a total stranger, who looked young enough and strong enough to be the ax murderer. (Man, several years ago I was all-hours victim to accounts of boogeymen on this wind-riddled spit of remote earth, one thing that did encourage me to read: you keep reading to stay awake and so get a good jump if the Hook Man breaks in.)

He stepped in. She stepped back. "In the name, it would seem, of paralegal service," she said, and turned and walked away and crossed the living room and sat on the creaking wicker sofa on her legs, "you have done me a *grave* disservice." She said this in her explicatory, cadenced style, punctuated and metered so no idiot could fail to record it in his notebook. The stranger, who had not followed her, then looked at me, evenly and without expression. He came in.

"My maid has quit," she said.

"I have not served anyone yet," the stranger said.

"You wanted her daughter, anyway. I am now without retainer. Do you paralegals make restitution of damages such as retiring twenty-year employees?"

"Do you know where her daughter is?" He sat down.

"Do you want to find out?"

Here they stopped. I could see his back, arms on his knees; he was sitting looking directly at her. She had her drink. She looked over the rim of it at him, sort of looking out the tops of her eyes and hiding her mouth with the drink.

"If you'll tell me, I'll get the other one back," he said.

"No, you won't. You won't even find her."

"Lately I am a professional at finding—"

"You won't find her unless I tell you where she is, and you probably won't find her daughter unless *she* tells you where *she* is."

"Where did she go, then?"

"That's a laid-low to catch a meddler."

"A what?"

"Skip it. I'll tell you what. Since you scared hell out of my maid and my estate is consequently short-handed, you might assist me . . ." She kind of trailed off.

They looked at each other a while.

"If you want to find either of them, you might hang around a bit."

"Hang around?"

"I am short on domestics, it would seem. There's the gardening and the brass polishing, of course, but as a coachman . . . And Simons has just today manifested a problem in his school-bus riding. You could escort him to school and back, and keep up the quarters on the beach, and let me see if I can locate Athenia for you."

"I suppose I might," he said.

"And could you tell me what *is* paralegal service?" She knew what it was. The old man was a lawyer and every joe to take her out since who wasn't a professor was an ambulance chaser or coroner. She was not asking to get an answer, but to know the answerer. This tactic was used when she had brilliant students over, mostly.

The stranger accepted the game. She was still accelerating, ever since the door, and virtually beaming at him over the whiskey, her tawny old Kool-Aid.

"That straddles law and law *enforcement*," he said, and I was certain, without any evidence, that he was grinning. He had passed a little test with flying colors—not flinched at all the crap about servants and brass polishing, but accepted her game, and what her game was even I did not know. But I knew something was going on, and if I had not been buzzing on Empirin, I could have told whether it was really going on, or just me, buzzing on Empirin.

"Well," the Doctor said, in her summing-up tone, "there's a cake down there. Send it back with Simons. Can you walk okay, Ducks?"

"Yes ma'am," I said.

I beat him out the door into the trees, leaning with the night wind away from the beach, and headed us for Theenie's shack. It was my birthday and I had a cake.

An Assessment of the Stranger

꙱ / Our beach is steep and not white but cochina. We took the fronting road, named Juno Boulevard by the speculator who sold his model-home land office to the Doctor. It is a mod building: an octagonal pagoda on stilts with two levels of parapet walks and sliding glass doors all around, a cupola on top with a widow's walk, all of it squatted over five thousand dollars' worth of heating and cooling equipment on a slab below, which would flood out with the first good blow. The Doctor got it for a price so famously cheap that everyone still shakes his head about it, but I don't know the exact amount. She caught him depressed.

The speculator bought a two-square-mile patch of desert, evenly between Savannah and Charleston, and figured to civilize it with fifty miles of city-block roads and sell it to the next wave of vacation-house affluents. He named the streets for the fifty states and those left over for their capitals. And the road on the beach, behind the first stand of dunes, he called Juno Boulevard, he told the Doctor, "for the moon." When the moon is up on this coast at this deep beach, it pours forth a hot glassy triangle over the sea, spreading just enough to illuminate both the land office and the maid's quarters if you stand between them. At that point facing inland you can see on the left the spectacular Mars-like edifice the Doctor got cheap and named the Savannah Cabana (her version of This'ldu or Here 'tis) and which probably helped secure for her the designation "Duchess" by the locals, and on the right a regular human shack, never moved or destroyed by the developer because he never sold or came close to selling the lot it was on. The Doctor told him she would need servants' quarters, and he threw that lot into the deal as well. I believe it was the only two lots he sold. Then the bank called in the paper.

The shack was stifling, with mosquitoes. Someone left the door open. In those days it was bug-tight, relatively speaking. Here, where the greatest natural resource is a toss-up between sand flea and mosquito, a thing is bug-tight if you do not die of a fever.

"Stand back," I told our new livery man. "I got to gun these things." I pulled the sprayer from under Theenie's bed, one of those old underslung can types with a slide plunger you can aim like a rifle. He not only stepped back, he went out and got some whiskey from his car.

Later we cut a hole in the windward side for the romantic view of the sea and perverted the genius of the builder. For this undoing there was no atonement. The original shack, by the grace of common sense, had faced inland, not romantically seaward, and when we got the boys' club spirit, combined with my dreamy horseshit ("We need a *Weltanschauung!*" I said), and cut a four-by-four hole, we invited an unstoppable, hourly legion of stinging pests into the shack and there was no screening them then, they could just let the wind push them gently through the wire like little hungry Houdinis, so we only put up shutters, iron-hinged, green, warped things Taurus got from Charleston, for larger pestilence, like hurricane.

But in those days if the door was shut it was all right. The stranger slapped himself a few times.

"The Cook's tour," I said.

"Wait." He poured out four inches of his whiskey in a jelly glass and drank an ice-water gulp. "Okay."

"This is it," I said, sweeping the room with my hand. It had the order of a Negro maid: things are not out of place but they are so crowded together that what is actually a tight bit of stacking at first looks random. The bed has four blankets, each turned down more than the one beneath and each a new color—blue and brown and yellow and red—giving a crowded, messy look to the neatness of a hospital-cornered bed. A small brown radio is at a perfect angle to the listener on the bed, but it struggles on the nightstand with a Mason jar and a Jesus, and shoeboxes full of folded papers are stacked on chests, doilies are everywhere, a religious velvet painting, on the windows see-through curtains, throw rugs on the floor. The room could be a museum exhibit obliged to have everything one old

black woman could have or could be known to ever
have had, a composite picture of the known habitat
of the Negro maid. And smells like a washed dog.
It was a mosaic, because if you stood too close it
looked just stuffed together, odd pieces of all manner
of cheap human conveniences glued into the room.
But if you looked at it as a whole, the picture had
an elegant form, was a spare machine of necessary
items for a lone person to live in a single room.

He pushed the jelly glass a half foot toward me on
the enameled metal table, white with a cobalt trim.
I sniffed at it and took a sip and wheezed. He smiled,
reading the newspaper on the walls.

I got the cake, still in its pan, and was ready to
go when something made me slow down. The
Doctor had engaged this man to chauffeur me,
had easily granted him Theenie's place on the
assumption she was gone and he was responsible—
what was going on? In their little compact it looked
like they knew more than I did, a regular thing for
the adults, but now I was being asked to comply with
this common understanding that welcomes a process
server into what passes for the family unit as the
Doctor and I know it. The Boy Act is the best thing
when in doubt. "You want to look through the
telescope?" I said.

"If you do," he said.

Curious bird, I thought, taking my leave. "Wait
here." I run down—time for another Empirin, the
ribs are starting to creak again—and drop off the
cake and get my telescope and go back. The Doctor
got it to go with the old, varnished, cigar-brown

globe she got me that you can't see any particular
country on, and the telescope does match: you can't
see anything particular with it either. It is brass and
the old glass optics have something in them like
cataracts, but for occasions like this one it serves
fine. I pulled this number on one of the Doctor's
suitors once, a coroner named Cud, vulture of a
fellow circled around for weeks before I got rid of
him with a telescope stunt. It came very natural then.
I was hiding in my room, mostly from him, because
the Doctor was gone and I didn't care to talk to him,
but he's there, waiting for her, and my door opens
and I grab the first prop available, which is the scope.
I hunk down on it out of reflex and the coroner says,
"How's the weather?" Again out of reflex, so I don't
reveal any idleness in my apparent absorption with
the view, I hunk down as if glued to something
fascinating. I am impervious, so great is the vision.
I fix my eyeball airtight on the ocular lest he see a
point to invite himself on in with.

"See any pirate ships out there?" he says (vomit)
and I screw down so hard that the surf I'm aimed at
is falling slow and fast and is gray and another
gray, then becomes, like, colors, tumbling corpuscles
of TV snow, which become blue and yellow and then
purple and red, and then shapes begin to appear
within a field of the tumbling colors.

Anyway, these cloud shapes start moving around
in the view, irregular and flowing, about like when
you press your eyelids. And one of them looks like
a clipper ship, so I tell the coroner named Cud: "I
see clipper ships at 0–9–2." Then go purple in my

descriptions. Well, it worked like a charm. He was gone, as I recall, before the Doctor returned. And it occurred to me after that that it was a nifty little adult gauge, a feeler, that telescope.

But this night was a hint different. The Empirin had my tongue like a grit of sand in an oyster of nonsense, and this stranger was no Cud going to hightail because of a little imagination in the family.

I set it up outside, where the mosquitoes were less dense, and addressed the view like a mariner, legs wider than the brass tripod. I give it the old hunk, then a little juke one way, another hunk. "Oooo," I let out, a little cat moan over the surf, choirboy. Then I start tracking. "Clippers." He just stands there and looks out at the Atlantic.

"Some fetching old Yankee Doodles, yessiree." He has not flinched. "Here. You look." I stepped back, careful to hold the telescope on line, nodded to it. "Come on, hurry, they're at good speed."

The stranger took the scope. "I don't see them."

I figured the test about over, but I threw in one more thing. "More south. They're not called clippers for nothing."

"No," he said, "not clippers for nothing."

"Tell me what you see."

He sighed, and then he jerked the scope a half inch to the right and froze it. Looking back on it, this is where I place his biggest gamble, his shrewdest moment. "Tell me, what should I see?"

"Clippers!" I exhaled. "Wooden laminate masted rolling regular clippers!"

He grunted and shuffled his feet.

"The canvases are coarse," I say. "Shredded and hemp-flogged, *wet*, salt-stained, grand pieces of cotton representing the lost fields who bore them!"

"Yes," the stranger said.

"Muslin!" I nearly shout. Who was testing who? "Great flying manila, popping in the breath of Neptune. And the *wood*. Varnished hard and sleek, teak and oak. The grains are a study."

"A what?"

"Check the hulls!" He just looked on, patient as ever. "Well?" I had him.

He blurted, "The hulls. Yes." He got away with something again! This really set me up. I turned the vertical-hold knob.

"And the paints, marine paints, coat on coat, voyage on voyage, haul, haul, dry haul diurnal and long. The colors are myriad and embattled, layered soldiers on the land it is their end to protect: blues, yellows, marine greens, and reds barnacled all over each other in their hopeless flaking mission. They've had it, bleached christenings of some jack-leg lubber in . . ." I was spent. Where had my boats been painted?

"Savannah," he said, still looking.

We looked over the water where the pattern of infinite shatterings forming the bright, glassy triangle from the moon was unbroken by boat or bird.

"I'm Simons," I said. We shook hands.

"When it's school time you'd better come get me," he said.

"All right. You want to tell me about this Theenie thing?"

We went in the shack and he poured himself another jelly glass of liquor and my own little wheeze of it and told me what happened. And a few other things I wanted to know, and more in the morning and afternoon, and we began our association thenceforth.

A Summons at Edisto

❧ / The process server told me he took the coastal highway south and the small road off to the left at a sign marked Edisto Beach. For twenty miles he drove in the dark to the steady sound of his automobile. Then he began to hit the marsh pockets.

He could not see the beginning marshes but could hear them. The cruising fullness of sound made by his car noises bouncing back from the close oaks and country houses would suddenly stop; a hollow, retreating, new quiet air. He looked out and saw nothing and then house and brush and trees blasted back close and full of sound. It was like running through an old wooden house, rooms opening off a narrow hall, hollows of sound breaking the noise of your running.

It was too late to serve a paper. He stopped and stayed in a motel that sat in a halo of its own pink-and-green neon lights. In the small wooden room, he went to sleep listening to the hypnotizing hum of cars down the road.

In the morning all he had to go on was an account of a set of roads near the beach beyond the paved road. There were miles of them, and on one of them, near the beach, was what was described to him as a rich man's house. Near it was a small shack. There his trail ended. He had a summons for a woman someone said had something to do with that shack.

Coming around a curve in the road where oak trees were painted white, he had to stop because of people in the road. He parked his car and got out and walked toward a tree they were surrounding. "Law," one of them said. Looking through them, he saw at the foot of the tree a boy, as if asleep, suddenly open his eyes and jump up, as if awakened. Then the boy sat down.

He shouldered back through the crowd past a school bus and continued. The air was salty as he reached the end of the hard road and began nosing down a graded road through heavy palmetto. The palmetto grew fuller, became a virtual tunnel of scabbling palms. He passed a wooden sign, SAVANNAH CABANA, and then saw the rich man's house. He got out and climbed its stairs and knocked and looked in. In the main room were wicker sofas and chairs, a bamboo bar, a ceiling fan, metal tumblers, and glass decanters. The long curtains suspended over the floor-to-ceiling windows kept billowing out with the breezes, dusting the hardwood floors. The place was lit by the ocean's bright upward glare. He went down the stairs and saw, beside a rusted-out Carrier compressor, a heap of carpets housing sea roaches and sand crabs.

He pulled up to the other, smaller house up the beach. The door opened and an old Negro woman said, "Sim, your momma was'n spose—" and stopped, eyes lowering. "What you wont?"

"I'm looking for Louester Samuels."

She looked at him in wonder. She managed to say, "What you wont wid her?"

"It's a legal paper for her."

"I know what you wont," she then said, and fell back into the small house and grabbed a shawl and a stack of linen and nearly knocked the process server down with her charge out the door. Then she turned and circled him and went back in and pulled a bundt pan from the oven bare-handed and charged him again. Then she stopped and dropped the cake on a table and made a final charge past him and down and out and trundled to the first tunnel of palms husking in the wind and stopped and turned and she fixed him with an incredulous look. Then was gone into the queer, muffling, constantly moving trees. The process server stood on the porch under an overhang of tin roof, its wood hot and dry from the long afternoon sun, the tin going *tic, tic*.

He went inside and smelled the hot cake and looked the room over. What took his attention was the walls, covered with yellowed newspapers. He read them, kneeling on the bed to get closer—stories about the Work Projects Administration. He felt the bed, soft in its heavy blanketing, and lay down and crossed his feet and put his hands back under his head and took a nap.

He woke a little after dark and left the house for

the husking tunnel of palms and palmettos the Negress had taken. At its end was the other house, the Savannah Cabana. He climbed the stairs again and stood on the porch beside a wringer washing machine until a woman came to the door.

That's the bare bones of how he scared Theenie out of the county. What took me some time to figure out was why. She thought he was her grandson. That's what the Doctor said, anyway. It sounds crazy, because he looks as white as a regular coroner to me. But you know how that works.

I remembered then that Theenie used to complain about her daughter being in trouble. In Theenie's book you can be dead broke, sick, jobless, no place to stay, and still be doing all right provided the law is not after you. She calls it the gubmen. The gubmen is like God: all-powerful and merciless. The hardest thing in the world for her to do is call the social security office about a late check. If she had one stolen from her mailbox, I'm not sure she'd call anybody. "Life hard, Sim" is about what she'd say. And hire someone to watch for the postman next time.

And the Doctor said she thought this process server was her grandson by her daughter who went to New York, which is Gomorrah to people here. Well, one look at him and you knew he was not *all* black, and that meant white people were involved, and one look at his blue summons and she knew the gubmen was involved, so it's major.

A Question of Heredity

🌸 / It didn't take a genius to know it was big, not after I knew Theenie had been at the house and thrown down the laundry and wasn't back at her shack and had left my cake out there without her wax paper sealed to it like peritoneum—you know, she has a thing about freshness. She can sit down with some chicken she found in tin foil about two weeks old and heat it up by letting it sit on the table while she irons and then eat it with a Co'-Cola, bouncing the bones in her hand to check for meat she hadn't sucked off, and be perfectly happy. And she could cook mullet brought in head down in a pickle bucket of pink fish slime and worm goo, fry them, and bounce those bones a little too, but when it comes to making something like a cake, which, considering its components (like water and flour and other powders), can't be too foul, at least not like mullet in a bucket sat on by a fat lady in the sun until they stopped biting—it comes to making a bakery-clean white thing like a cake and she's got to have fresh eggs, fresh real butter, sweet milk, and you can't even walk around the house while it cooks lest it fall, and she won't run the vacuum cleaner while it's in there either. She can only sit down with another Co'-Cola and a Stanback powder to virtually pray for it, and then it's out, it will have to cool, and nine times out of ten, before you can touch it, she has grafted to it wax paper set into the hot buttery sugary crust of the cake and welded there by a fusion of wax and cake, and that cake you could throw in the ocean and it would float like a crab-pot marker for years, and the day it washed up on a beach and was found by an islander he could take it to his hut and with great-eyed delight peel off the wax paper with his skinning knife and devour the rich, golden flesh inside. And as soon as you slice up this memorial, this baby, and make your smacky fuss about how good it is, she starts making her fuss about how much trouble it is, and she's not making any more, she's too old, you're too old, too old for *her* to have to work that hard, why, she *raised* you. (She raised two other sets of white kids before me. And she's not through until she hears they got married.) You smile and smack and smile away, she sitting at the kitchen table in her white uniform, hair bluing and legs swollen, fingering an aspirin onto a toothache, complaining and complaining before rising and completing without another idle breath the rest of the cleaning or ironing or bed-making or whatever kind of tracking after the mess of white folks that afternoon presents, and she shows up the next morning with a silent assault on the breakfast detail, fresh and renewed somehow against a thousand cigarette butts in amber dregs of whiskey, and strewn clothes, and crap, crap from the high life.

So I knew it didn't take no genius to know something big was about, and from the way the Doctor took in Taurus like the bright kid they'd heard had decided to be an English major, from the way she toyed with him, the crap about servants, his hanging around, an obvious bid for a surrogate father for me—it isn't the first time she has solicited the attentions of your notably masculine types, at least partly I am sure for some father image around the house—and from what Taurus told me about her (Theenie) bolting out of the shack with jets of terror into the palms waving around like big testifying arms at a revival, from this I knew something was up, particularly for Theenie, old Theenie, who says to me, "Sim, you ain't *got* to do but two things. One is die, and thuther is live *till* you die." I turn my head like a beagle at the novelty of this suggestion coming from her. "Ain' I right?" she says. "I guess you are," I say. "You *believe* it, then."

And I suppose you begin to. You certainly have to think she must believe it, odd as it seems at first that she can believe she has freedom, but then it looks like that belief might be her support in her heavy old world. She must say deep down somewhere very quietly while standing on those swelling brown-scaled legs ironing again and again the brocade this, the fancy that, that she can stand it, stand the steam rising off the board into her face, hot fingers manipulating the coverlets and slipcases just out of range of the iron, steam rising to her sweaty face before the fan turns and blows it off her, because she doesn't *have* to, she likes Simons, he all right, but I ain' got to do it for him neither, I *will* is all. I only got to do two things. Die and live till.

So what makes her pour out of her house and job like water downhill because a man who might be a simple bill collector, some fool, interrupts her at cake baking?

You don't ask an old soothsayer like Theenie herself, who in this case could not be asked because she didn't stop running, save for the brief talk she had with the Doctor, until she got safely back on John's Island. You ask a great old earthy philosopher like Theenie something truly mysterious too directly and the answer you get, if you get one, will be as evasive as your question was blunt. I'm sitting on the commode one day and look off at the trash can by my knee and see some gauze, a bandage, and open it up and there's blood on it, with black flecks like pepper in it—I about faint. "Theeeenie!" I yell. "Thee*nee*!" I'm buckling up in a white fine sweat and pointing at the can when she opens the door. "Who got cut?"

"Hmmp!" she says. "No one." And slams the door, leaving me there in the surgical chamber.

That leaves the Doctor sole heiress to the fortune of secrecy that has her quietly jubilant about losing her maid and welcoming into the house *the* man who chased off her maid, and she gives him the maid quarters when he doesn't ask for them, and charges him with taking me to school. It leaves the Doctor, who had quite a little chat with Theenie, it would seem.

There was nothing for it but direct questions, no one but the new man and the Doctor to ask.

"How'd you scare her that bad?"

"I don't know."

"See you tomorrow."

I took my cake back to the Cabana, where the Doctor was perfectly blumbery. I took her drink and freshened it without being asked (she holds the glass out and says, "Do me?").

"How come that dude scared Theenie?"

"Have you been writhing?"

"Yes ma'am, a whole story just today. But tell me how he scared her."

"She believes she's her grandson—he's. *He's* her grandson. He's come to avenge them for leaving him in New York."

"Who?"

"Her daughter. Her daughter and she did."

"A *baby*?" I asked. Didn't sound like Theenie at all.

She nodded.

"Because he was not . . ."

"Half," she said. "And she says it was sick. Anyway, I'm not sure she's right."

"But she's scared," I said.

"Yes, she's scared," she confirmed, with a slow, exaggerated nodding of her head.

"Well, good night."

"Sleep tight," she said. "Sweet dreams." It wouldn't do to ask any more. I can make it up just as true as she can. So I got out my spiral notebook and corrected for the lie I told about writing a story that day.

BETWEEN LIVING AND DYING
by Simons Manigault

Between living and dying, she had made two mistakes. One was letting her daughter go to New York to be a singer, and the other was letting them take her daughter's baby from its grandmother, herself, who got there in time to get it and take it home and raise it right, whether he was half white or not and sick. It was the sick that got him away from her, the sick that her daughter gave it, junk in it. Her daughter in New York messed up on drugs and taking things called fixes got the baby away from her and got her half convinced he was going to die so she let them take him and then she was never able to get him back and her fool daughter crazy enough to go to a place like that was too crazy to want him if she could have had him and she was just an old colored lady a long way from home and she left. It grinded her up to think about it and she never forgot it and she knew it was not true about having only to die and live till you die. You had to be careful somewhere in between or you could be chased by something like losing your daughter's baby because you weren't careful somewhere else, and you lost your daughter herself or she lost her sense, which is the same. You could be chased by it and even caught up with.

And it would come for you, not your daughter who had no sense, but you who did, who knew better all along, you the wrong one in it. You would have to leave Simons and Mizmanigo and weave baskets again, but that would be the price.

So Theenie and Taurus never talked, not after her terrible recognition, trundling *kawhoosh* past him, floorboards bending and springing her off the porch over the steps she would have stumbled down, her crooked-worn and polished pump heels flying in the sand. And her turning the yellow-and-white eyes on him for one last look and whirling at last into the ushering arms of the rat palms. I call them rat palms because we were pulling them off, the dead butts of branches, one night for a fire, and because you must pull very hard to rip them loose, I learned the hard way that whatever is between the husk and the coconut-hair bark of the tree comes down on your arm, and that night in the dark my whatever-in-between was no drowsy rumpled sparrow or polite silken tree frog but a rat about the size of possum and texture of armadillo, and it landed all over my arm from hand to shoulder in one shuddering rush, and I nearly shook my arm out of socket and got a chronic case of girls' fear of rats from that and still have it, and you would too.

So he goes in the house and reads W.P.A. stories on the walls where the roaches have eaten away the flour but not the ink of the newspapers, and he naps, wakes, and emerges into the old, bored heat of this named but never discovered small place of the South and hears the tin roof *tic*, *tic* in that heat.

So they never talk. One runs calf-eyed into the woods from the other, who later watches her on Sony monitors in a wall bank of federally funded TV sets. *On a tape* he sees what he sees of her, what he sees of—I found out—of his only known or at least speculative origins, watches as calmly as a surgeon an operation.

What would she have told him if she could have

stayed? Probably the usual speech she would make to coroners courting the Doctor.

"She got a *double* use for *you*, mister. If you cain' see that, why you scudgin' us all. Ever since Mr. M. left, it's been a trile with that Simons. Because iss onliess us here. He roundbunction, *in* trouble, fallin' out of *buses*, *ekk*setra. All she wont is somebody to keep him right. Even *she* know that. And Law knows I do, I see enough of that in my own. Somebody got to hep that boy kotch up. He so far ahead he's *behine*. Yes, he *is*." Her head nodding, in a rhythm like a small, gentle locomotive; her whole head rolling on the syllables. "Yes*suh*."

A fine speech and well-intended. But she'd tell it to every coroner and tennis attorney aiding and abetting Arabs to come around here. A wonderful bunch of suitors. Penelope never figured on such a healthy run of dudes when the Progenitor bagged it, I hope.

Taurus came in the house, played a game, accepted an invitation to spend a while with us, told me everything I asked, and otherwise kept his eyes open and his mouth shut. He was somebody you figured knew something. And he was supposed, as Theenie would have put it, to "rescure" me.

I was going to have to modify the Boy Act. He was definitely modifying the Coroner Act.

We See a Fight in Charleston

✤ / I told him nothing ever happens here but he wouldn't listen, and couldn't we hike in the woods, he wants to know. The woods, I say. What woods?

"All that dark close noise I passed coming down here," he says. "The black changing sound."

So I had to tell him they was no woods, they was leftovers.

"From what?"

"From, number one, from nothing happening to them except heat and afternoons of Negroes in white shirts with their eyes turning yellow looking at the road. And from, two, from the heat and the rain making so much grow that since no planters or even Sherman ever got here to weed anything out, it became a giant unpruned greenhouse festering in its very success," I said. "Burning up in an excess of youth, like city slums," I said. "Only this city is a rich unturned city of no lights.

"And it became a bog of verdure and got scurvy

sort of and the big oaks became turkey oaks and the palm trees became palmettos, and *then* the Arabs landed.

"And they bought the choicest squats what were touched by wind or water, and hired some American scalawags who somehow got that tennis-ball-velvet grass to grow on sand and so converted sand dunes to sand traps, and they cemented the rest and painted it green and so the tennis pros showed up next (not the big ones, only ones like Rod Laver and I saw a college kid beat him), and then the tennis groupies in their German cars and then the Germans themselves came, BASF chemical conglomerate, but an old-time referendum took care of them and sent them home. They didn't hide their intentions.

"So after the tennis groupies got moved into their exclusive condominia, their dogs came, replacing the natural old squatters like skunks and possum with Irish setters, a new breed of them that ignores birds for Frisbees, and then they shored it all up with fake redwood and yardmen disguised as gardeners and attorneys as world travelers on their sailing yachts that never leave the marina. That leaves the scurvy woods and the rickets people right where they were. Right here."

We had walked into this anemic scrub a ways. Before us I showed him an old homesite I call the Frazier ruins.

"Because I forgot a few details," I said. "Before the Arabs, but in the same choice sites they bought, the Marines bought the very first island, and for one

simple and sufficient reason: it contained an ade-
quate, maybe the largest, population of the region's
first and final indigenous denizen: the sand flea. So
grunts get out there on Parris Island at attention
and they tell them not to move a muscle on pain of
whomp upside the head, and they become hamburger, and it probably won World War II. Because
sitting in a foxhole with Jap bullets zinging all over
Guam or shooting a flame thrower into a cave or
walking waist-deep over a half mile of razor coral
reefs because the LSTs ran aground and seeing half
of you shot wasn't as bad as doing pushups in sand
fleas, so we won.

"And one other detail. Joe Frazier."

The homesite was little pine trees coming up
through powdery old two-by-fours and rusty tin
panels in the hot sand. Taurus was already looking
at the skinks. Skinks are lizards made for speed.

"And the skinks." He already knew how to hold
them in place with eye contact. You can walk right
up on skinks sometimes if they know you are looking
right at them and you do not break eye contact,
but if you look away to take a step, they are gone,
because they know you don't know which way they
went.

"This could have been where he trained," I said.

"Who?"

"Frazier."

"Oh."

"Maybe right under this tin is the rotten old
croker sack, just resting in the sand after the hard
work of getting Joe on his way to Everlast leather
bags and Philadelphia and the big time and—"

"What croker sack?"

He stopped me, but of course he didn't really want to know. I think he hadn't been paying attention to me. And he was right: Who knows if Joe hit a croker sack? He might have just torn up a nightclub or something and somebody got him to a gym in time to put his natural destructiveness to work. But the time I took a Dixie cup of the Doctor's Early Times out here to see what she saw in it, I was sure about Joe and the bag.

He was at the bag in his snot-dauber routine. On a short arm of rope swayed the bag, as large and solid as a piece of ocean, as heavy as tide. Joe hit it and it veered and he blew snot out of his left nostril and hit it coming back and stopped it still. Joe got on a bus. The bag hung there, the beam held it, the barn held on, the town, the heat. The green browned, Joe won.

In Philadelphia they had canvas bags with pockets worn in them by professional punches. They tied a rope across the gym chest-high to Joe and made him step across the gym under it, bobbing from side to side. They said, "Touch it with your ears, Frazier, but don't make the rope move or you'll do it all day." Joe got so good and fast at it that it sometimes seemed the rope moved, not his head, like you think only the cloth moves but a sewing machine needle doesn't. He got so good he threw in extra touches: rolled his shoulders, hooked the snot off his nose, went *hinh hinh* to keep time, faked and mimicked punches. Off this motion would spin his success, would come long looping punches that would have busted croker sacks to pieces. The rope was steady;

he followed it. It led him to the Heavyweight Championship of the World. The liquor didn't make me numby or anything, but I did eat the wax out of the Dixie cup, which was a childhood thing of mine, and the liquory, stainy wax tasted much better than the snort itself.

"You want to see him fight?"

"What?" I said. "Who?"

"Frazier."

"Where?"

"Charleston."

"Sure if we—"

"I'll get tickets."

I was a goofball not to know about the fight; it was the Ali fight. Taurus just stood there in the sun, smiling. We walked all over the ruin, the tin breaking in great *ka-thunks*, spurting the skinks out of and back into their jillion million corrugated bunkers. The little bastards had it made: pinstriped miniature monitor dragons, gun-blue survivors, pen-and-ink leftover pygmies of the dinosaur days, living in modern galvanized tunnels buried in the sand like long Quonset huts shrunk down so small even the government lost them.

We drove half the night that night, up Highway 17, watching all the flintzy old motels with names like And-Gene Motel that are about closed for good since I-95 opened up and drained the blood out of the old roads. And clubs, or joints, or *jernts*, the Negroes say, umpteen eleven jernts with neon tubes running all over them, broken so the color and the

gas leaked out with the road blood. It's very sad.
There's one place built like a mosque or something,
with this bulbous outline like a fancy sundae, and
the neon still works: purple and red. We stopped
to get some beer because Taurus said you needed
beer to go to a fight because you had to understand
the people who might get carried away after it and
start a fight with you. In the jernt was a gritty floor
and a jukebox and some red booths. A woman in
tight black pants and a red stretchy shirt sitting by
the cash register got the beer, took the money, rung
it in, got back on the stool, picked up a cigarette,
blew smoke up at the ceiling, and we left.

Well, I took one. Taurus looked in the sack when
I did, as if to count the remainder, but he didn't say
anything.

It was awful, but I used it to hurry up and get
there with.

We stopped at the Piggly Wiggly and got some
food. They had Hoppin' John so I got some in a
square carton with a nifty wire handle and intricate
closing designs cut into the flaps like a goldfish carton at a fair.

We finally got there. It was in a gym, a big blood-
colored thing probably built by the W.P.A., because
it had those heavy, square, useless blocks of stone
all over so you couldn't tell if it was a museum or
what. It was as big as an airplane hangar, with third-
story windows they open with chains and pulleys
from the floor, and fans in the windows the size of
propellers.

Five thousand people were in there on bleachers

and metal folding chairs around a boxing ring in which a Negro who looked like a moose was trying to box a pink-white dude with a snow-white flat-top haircut. I say white, but he had green-and-blue tattoos all over his body—a standing bruise. I never had seen any real boxing before and what got me was how nobody seemed to get hit and they spent a lot of time hugging each other until the referee would tell them none of that. The Negro was as big as James Earl Jones and as bald and looked scared, and the white man was bobbing all the time and sliding and grinning all the while like he knew a private secret.

"The black guy's with the promoter's stable," Taurus told me.

"Stable?" I said. "Like horses?"

"The other guy's from prison."

"You mean like Sonny Liston? He learned to box there and got out—"

"No," he said. "He's *in* there. He lives there."

"How do you know?"

"I saw their bus."

"Wha'd it say?"

"C.C.I."

"Charleston Cornhole Idiots."

"Columbia Correctional Institution."

Well, that made all the difference in the world. Now I saw the white guy's secret. He was grinning because he was on the town, out of stir for the night, chained up and bused down and unchained for a night of freedom. And the Negro twice his size was scared because he was in the ring with a *convict*.

Behind the boxers loomed an almost drive-in-sized luminescent screen, white as the moon. The real fight would come on that. You could see a big cable running across the floor away from it that I guess the broadcast had to come through. The moose and the bruise performed their bobbing and hugging, their tiny terrors like mortal shadows against the very sky.

"What's that fireman doing here?"

"He's the fire marshal. I don't know."

We watched the fire marshal talk to a dude with pointy shoes and skinny pants near the door. Then the dude sort of held his hands up in the air and pushed it several times like he was saying "All right" or "Calm down" to the fireman. Then the fireman left and they began closing the doors, but people pushed through. Then they locked them with chains around the handles, the bar kind you press to open school doors. People hit the doors with chairs, which you could tell were chairs because their legs came popping through the glass, that thick, glue-colored glass in school doors with chicken wire set inside. It sounded like guns.

When the first flicker of light hit the screen, it threw up the boxers' shadows bigger than Olympic giants and the whole crowd shut up. Like that. We must have looked like a photograph of a crowd, faces silent, still, looking through blue cigarette smoke.

One more tiny flicker and the hum-drum cranked up louder than ever and I didn't hear any more chairs go off. It flickered a bunch and the fighters started sort of ducking from the light, crouching down and taking a peek at the screen so not to miss anything.

When it flickered off they were huddled in a little clench, taking a peek, and when it came on it cast their shadows up on the screen, and we laughed, because you'd see tiny mortals in a huddle and then they'd start fighting and it would come on and they'd be bigger than Godzilla for a couple of crazy, huge hooks; then sloppy amateurs again, then *bir*UP: Killers on the Skyline, the biggest sluggers of all time.

The crowd started booing, so the promoter threw in the towel on his moose, who was glad, and they got out of the ring and everyone just watched the screen. A second or two of faraway light like heat lightning kept hitting it, notching up the noise with every moon-like vision; the audience a bunch of primitives getting giddy because they can't figure out the television, don't know whether to watch the fantastic little men *in* it or to watch *it*, weirded out by the promise of the spectacle but also by this queer satellite light or whatever pouring a faraway world into this hot, smoky gym.

A flash of something real: Ali! and cheers go up. Coppery and gliding, done up in white shoe tassels, eyes bright as a squirrel's, dancing like skip-to-the-music. Those tassels whipping around, wrapping and unwrapping, cracking like whips, *violent*-looking things, snapping and fibrous and lashing his solid legs. You can't hear yourself.

And Joe! *Louder* cheers. He chugs in wearing pedal pushers, big green paisley bloomers, already snot-daubing, a million hunkering little ducks and hooks in the perfect rhythm of the taut rope, buoy down and buoy up, and *hinh* and *hinh*, Joe's got the sound going already.

"You know what he is?" I say.

"Who?"

"He's a renascent smart ass."

Taurus looked at me.

"But now Joe," I said. "There is *business* in Joe." I had him smiling.

A rumor comes by that Joe's family is in the gym and people are looking for them, but fat chance of that because there's every dude with a wallet between Denmark and Olar in the joint, pimps and bankers and city *muh-fuh* gentlemen in colorful undershirts, and country cane pole ones in flannel shirts, but Taurus is looking at one bunch up top I decide might as well be them. There are three or four heavyset kind-of-old ladies in Cossack hats like fur bowls on their heads—probably their Sunday rigs. And behind them stand some men a bit younger and thin-looking in cigar-brown suits with their white shirts very bright, and dark, skinny ties. Their faces are dark and narrow too. Overall they look a bit unsure about things, like it's church.

That's about how Joe looks, bouncing in his corner as if he'd like to kneel down in a pew. And Ali orbiting, advertising, selling, leering like he ought to have on an Elvis Presley costume instead of a terry robe, and Joe snot-daubing, and if they were his people in there, they drove up in probably one big Buick and planned to drive all the way back that night just to see their boy on a drive-in movie screen beamed in by a radio contraption in space a million miles away, and Joe is worried about them driving that far, as if he doesn't have enough to worry about with, I have to admit, a majestic-looking machine of a man ass-holing all around the ring, and Ali, Mr. *ex*-Cassius Clay, is worried about a woman at ringside he's going to leave his sweet wife for named Veronica Porshe. I read that later.

Well, there's a bunch of circus barking, and *ding* and they're off. Whatever it is that goes on, goes on punctuated by *ding*s and the yelling becomes *who won that one i don't know i don't know either who won that one* and *ding* and yelling again. Five thousand fire-code violators yelling, elbowing, stomping, craning, holding their heads when they can't stand it, lusting for their chosen hero on this living moonscape of escape when—

Silence.

Ali is going over, going over like, like a tree—

All noise.

We see only then, before he hits the deck, Joe's extra-special message to Mr. Smart Ass, looping out of the dark like one of those mace balls, Ali's eyes skittering toward it white like a horse's. All the people are in the air.

In the air they grab each other and shake each other like their stepchildren, and make noise like children being shaken, hysterical garbling and nonsense, jerking each other silly, agape at a fallen god.

And Taurus wasn't even *looking*. He stood there as if an anthem were playing and looked at the Cossack ladies. And they were looking straight ahead, not at the screen.

"He *south*pawed him," I screamed, but he didn't seem to hear.

"I never knew what that word meant until—" But he wasn't listening.

We left and drove again, half until ever, and did not stop at a jernt or talk or anything, and I made it to school the next day on time.

How He Got His Name

✺ / It sounds funny, but I named him.
And it is less ridiculous, someone being named
Taurus, than you might think. The first night we
went to the Baby Grand together I named him.

We strolled in, I the homunculus, and he the true
circus property, because any dude that looks white
and walks into a sweet shop without the credential
of knowing someone *very* well or of wearing a
badge is like a circus clown and his safety will depend on the dudes deciding he *is* a clown. That is
what good race relations means. So we go on in past
Jinx and Preston at the pool table, and I supply a
nod up in the air while I walk and sort of overdo it
in order to point at Taurus without using the geek's
gesture of a direct indication—we walk right past
them like nothing's new. That casualness tells them
that I know him very well and they must continue
shooting pool not to blow protocol. They see I am
bringing an inside guest, not an outside guest, and

they must meet him as if at a big party, with gracious
informality, when they happen to find themselves
within speaking range.

It's a high show, because even though I am boy
wonder in here, the Duchess's little duke, I've never
brought a guest. In fact, the only whites I've ever
seen in the Grand are the old-family boys who come
in stoned and with goods to share when there's some
music. The Doctor could probably bring in a coroner,
but she wouldn't.

"Two 45s," I tell Jake.

He reaches down in the silver icebox and looks up
at us before hauling them up.

"*Cold* ones, now, Jake. My friend is *thirsty*." You
try to put the world in simple terms when it's
complicated.

Two tallboys hit the bar, sixteen ounces and long
as howitzer shells.

"Jake, want you to meet—"

They were ahead of me. Taurus had one hand
on his beer and the other up in the air, with his
elbow on the bar as though to arm-wrestle, and Jake
swung into it in the Negro sidewinder handshake.
They paused and Jake gave a most delicate knuckle
bump with his free hand before touching both his
hands to the bar rag tucked into his apron string.

"We heard you had a potner," Jake said to me.

Taurus watched us both.

"But I'm worrit about you bringin' him in *heah*."
Jake picked up the beers and wiped the water off
the bar and set them down. I was unsteady on my
stool, legs up in the air like one of the famous

Southern ladies whose feet never touch the floor
when they sit in chairs.

"Why?" I said.

"Cause if he tries to keep up wid *jew*, we mought
have to *care* him out," and he laughed his girlish
laugh, very artificial, very considerate: he was putting on a bit of the old nigger act while watching
my new potner. Everything would be fine.

"Jake," Taurus said, easily settling his can down
on Jake's side of the bar, "I would genuinely prefer
a *Slitz*, please."

"Malt?"

"Malt."

Jake got it. "Say, I know you take care of Sim and
no problem, iss no problem. He all reet."

"I got you," Taurus said then, split open his brand,
and he was in. *Slitz*—Jesus, he hit the dialect *and*
drank fast. It was then that I named him.

He set out for Preston and Jinx at the pool table
and I had to climb down the stool like Tarzan's boy
down a chrome vine. Just then two women came in
(you call them anything but that—sistahs, snakes,
or momma if the relationship is a close one) and
bumped into Jinx and Preston, who were turning
their backs to the front door to adjust for Taurus's
coming up to the table. Well, it would have been a
regular meeting like at the bar except the snakes
had action on their minds and saw Taurus with me
scrambling after him carrying a beer can as big
as my arm, and one of them said, hip-setting, "Who
dis?"

It was out before I thought to say it, with a certi-
tude that gave the name all the undeniability of a

flat, plastic decal across the rear windshield of a low
Buick: "Taurus. This is my fr—"

"Mistah *hoo*?" If a baby owl could hoot, it wouldn't
be any higher than that sound was. She was mock-
ing, of course, especially with the "Mister," but she
was interested enough to mock.

"Taurus," I said again. The miracle was, nobody
laughed.

"*Tau*rus?" the second snake said.

"Tau*rus*!" said the first. And he was veritably
laminated into the community, as easy as you please,
a fixture like me. I thought for a long time that it
went so easily because of my diplomatic powers and
immunities, that he moved like a fish in cool water
because I stocked the tank.

"This is Preston and this is Jenkins," I said.

"Preston," Taurus said, and shook Preston's arm
and looked into his eyes, which are like eyes deep
in a gorilla suit, and the same with Jinx, who is
more shy and whose eyes bulge out so he looks at
the floor to hide them.

"They call me Jinx," he said, and looked up.
Already Jinx's eyes had that liquid, yellow, mullet
look, from drinking too much that night and I guess
the nights before. Preston's were drier but too dark
and low to really tell. If there was ever a raid or a
fire or anything at the Grand, I thought Preston
would carry me out like I was Fay Wray and Jinx
would be caught rear guard—grabbed by his leg
going out a window or burned up. Of course I knew
everybody and they me, but these guys always seemed
genuinely happy to see me, unlike the others, and
Preston even understood what I meant when I

offered him my warm, undrunk 45s, and he drank them without a show of thanks, to preserve my reputation.

Cold air that night drove a bunch of people in, and everybody drank to keep warm, and Jake fried chicken wings half the night and kept putting beers and chicken wings in wax paper on the bar, and greasy faces and fingers took them. A deep press of people kept coming by and so everybody met Taurus in the party-decorous way, and late (kind of, for me) we got ready to go.

Taurus stopped and said to Preston on the way out, "Preston, I need you to do me a small favor. Tell Louester Samuels that I'm not going to serve her the paper about the mixup in Charleston. It went back to public service—the sheriff." Taurus walked out and Preston looked down at me.

"You know this Louester?" I said.

"Yeah, she heah now."

"She's *in* here?"

"She in heah, shihh. You saw her, first bitch in the door. He saw'm, too. Hell, Simaman, she momma work for you momma, if iss the right one."

"Well, I've never seen her, Preston."

"*He* know her?"

"I don't think so."

"He know sump'm. How he know I know her?"

"Later on, Preston. Later on."

The next day Taurus told me a couple of stories about serving paper and said it was good money on a loose schedule but he didn't like to do it. I thought they'd be good stories for the Doctor. But what got me that night was how he watched every-

thing and waited patiently for the moments to un-
fold before him. To the extent he lets me *name* him.
He never corrected me. I called him Taurus from
there on, fine with him. And little things like that
Slitz trick. He was controlling things, but like the
elephant promised the monkey, he wasn't going to
force it.

The Federal Oral History Program

☙ / "Take him to the museum," the Doctor told me, "and get those boys to show him the tape of her." She did not mean the Charleston Museum, a place where you can see all the birds east of the Mississippi preserved in these little bullet shapes like they were squeezed to death by the hand of, and rode in from the field in the pants pockets of, James Audubon himself, and kept in drawers like silverware after that, since about 1850 —I never thought about it before, but those could be antebellum birds. A *whale* is hanging from the ceiling, and drawing rooms cut out of local homes are in there too, whole complete rooms like they glued everything down and buzzsawed it loose from the Russell House or somewhere, and lugged it over and put little cards in it telling what everything was.

She meant the *art* museum. The best thing in that was the desk man, who sat stoned just inside looking at a Salvador Dali picture book, saying "Wow" very gently, and told you where you wanted to go in the museum, and whom past you could have carried any painting in there as long as you put the finished side at him so the gliding colors and lines would mesmerize him. But it wasn't the painting part we wanted anyway. We wanted the federal oral history program, which was in an outbuilding. That's where they had Theenie on a tape. Now I personally don't think Taurus needed to see her again, certainly not for the purposes the Doctor had in mind. Because he took the news that he was the Grandson of the Lost Nigger Maid so cool she thought he did not believe it, which most certainly was not the case. You could not say he believed anything and you could not say he disbelieved anything. He was a heroin baby, I told you that. I thought I made it up, but now I don't know. I may have heard it in the Doctor's relayed story. Once he told me he remembers very little of what happened before "last night."

"That's an exaggeration," I said.

"That's an exaggeration," he said. But he offered no more. And he never said his name was other than the tag I gave him, or where he came from, or why he was here.

What that means, a heroin baby, if he is one, I don't know, because my first and last brush with that stuff was reading the most genteel addict of all time's monograph, which the Doctor didn't have to tell me to read, because I got after that one on my own, thinking from the title it was going to present some titillating scenes of delectable and naked girls, which it did not. Everybody in that book sounded like these Dobermans I heard about at the Grand. They feed them ashes in their food, which somehow lowers the oxygen in their blood, and when they grow up they don't believe in anything, except maybe killing, and even the handler has to wear a football suit, more or less, and throw meat to wherever he wants them to go.

"Them Dobes light a nigga's ass *up*," Preston says.

Well anyway, it was something like these Dobes that happened to Taurus, which I say changed his whole approach to believing things. Like killing everything. Except his stance was more like killing nothing, as if he thought everything was alive or possible. It's hard to say. But I do know he did not *not* believe that Theenie was his grandmother any more than he did believe it, and so going for the Doctor's reason to see the tape was moot, but we went anyway, for the trip.

We went past the stoned dude down a hall with the two-tone wainscoting of green and lighter green —very soothing greens that they use in schools for hypers. Then we got to the studio.

In there on three walls were TVs banked into holes like microwave ovens, and all over the room, in strapped-up boxes with cables and ropes and wires and sockets and jacks all over them, was this Sony stuff—enough to, I swear, film a whole war. Half of it's on triangle dollies and tripods. I expected even a director's bullhorn.

Well, hidden down in this load are these two guys bent over a switch panel, messing with it, so that six of the TVs are on and President Nixon is talking on all of them. He says the same thing, but the angles are different and they're playing a sentence over and over and pointing at different screens. It's pretty obvious they're casing him for lies like

everybody does, even without forty-five TV sets. I
heard all that stuff.

Suddenly they turn around and look at us.

"Yes?" says one of them. I notice how pale and
zitty he looks for a college guy.

We don't say anything and their foreheads start
wrinkling up.

"Ye-yes?" he says again.

"Are you Bob Patterson?" Taurus says.

"It's Robert." He doesn't move toward us or anything, just says *It's Robert* like you'd say *It's candy*.

It's time for the Boy Act and a solid job of it too,
and before I knew it, I was acting like I had palsy
and stumbling around the room across these rivers
of technology, and going to try to hit his balls like
that midget at the cockfight. It was funny how fast
I was this pygmy wiseass, in a way that scared me
it was so thorough and deep and quick, and I can't
explain how I knew to do it or why I wanted to, but
I would have hit that bastard harder than a golf
ball, when Taurus has me by the back and holds me.

He has his thumb on my shoulder, his middle
finger down my back on the edge of vertebrae, and
he has a light frog on the muscle so I can't move
without getting a real frog.

"Well, Robert," he says, "Dr. Manigault sent us
to see one of your tapes."

"The famous basket tape," I said, and Taurus
frogged me so that I gargled a little trying to shut up.

"Oh yes," Robert Patterson said. "She did call."

Then he put his head in his hand and acted like
he had a headache. "It'll take us a while to find it.
It's not in our permanent collection." The other guy

got up and said he knew where it was and bumped into us, so they said we should stand outside until they got it set up, or until the second guy did, because he was the only one doing anything human.

So we waited in the hall. I knew of the tape but I'd never seen it. They got Theenie at the market weaving one Saturday when she was off, and I learned of it only because she wouldn't talk about it. The Doctor told me because they had had to have a man-to-man talk after it happened, to settle Theenie down. That was because Theenie somehow thinks TV is the law, and being on it is like being on trial or something. TV and the law are both these large things that are technical and controlled by white people, so it nerved her out.

I would tease her. "Hey Theenie, when's your show coming on?"

"What show?"

"Your TV show."

"Ain't no show."

"Well, I'm going to get me a *TV Guide* and find out."

"No you ain't. There ain't no show."

"I heard there was."

"Where you hear?"

"I heard is all. Like you do. From a little bud." She used to tell me she heard stuff about me from a little bird.

"Aw Got! Simons. Simons, why you wont to grind me up? You allus just *grinin'* me up." And here she would be about to cry, I swear, and I'd pull off surprised. I only did it twice, because it really did get to her. You could do the same thing by saying she had a phone call from a man about her social-security check and she'd start in on aspirin and leave early.

"I'm leaving, never coming back, Miz Manigault. Simons, that Simons is just *grinin'* me up . . ." And she'd leave ten minutes early and always be back. She could take any other teasing but the gubmen and the TV show.

They called us back in and we watched the tape. In the frame were tourists and baskets and then Theenie and her aunt—she calls her that but I think it's her neighbor—weaving, over against a wall. The second video lord, who was nice to us, is running over the baskets with an electric-shaver light-meter thing, poking it at everything. Then he gets this boom mike and says okay and the action starts. Then he leaves the frame and we hear a thump and *sound check sound check okay.*

So they had Theenie and her aunt there, all contained by those python co-ax and lesser electric mamba, afraid to move because of the equipment and the occasion. But they won't take any kind of picture guff except TV, which is too big to refuse, unless they are disoriented by having gone to Chicago or someplace when young, or somehow else got sophisticated. An integration program or two don't change a person's fundamental suspicion of film. It may even be old voodoo stuff.

Once we stopped on Meeting Street to get some flowers and a lady was selling baskets. The thing is, they always have about a thousand items arranged around them and they sit in some aspect of focus in the center or at a corner of the inventory and

weave *more*. You could run off with eighty pieces
before they could get up and shake off the marsh
grasses and throw the one-tined weaving fork at
you and call down Wrath. It wouldn't be pretty
when It caught up with you and the loot, sitting
around with eighty hot basket things you stole from
a woman. So no one ever tries it. They are so
confident—sitting and weaving, their whole *factory*
spread out, being walked on by tourists—they
watch only the present basket, reach into their
grocery sack beside the chair for new straw, and
answer questions.

"Ma'am, how much is this one?"

"Hum? Hum fuff-teen."

The basket is preciously set down.

"And this one?"

"Hum sebem."

Ah. The money begins to fish out and she stops
weaving. "Two for twelb." Consternation. But no.
One will do.

During the purchase a man with his family steps
up and says, "Ma'am, can I get a picture of you and
your work?"

She ignores him and he starts eyeballing with his
camera. "What choo wont?" she says.

"A picture—"

"You ain' *buyin'*."

"Well . . . no . . . I just—"

"Well, you got to be buyin'."

The first deal is still closing. The buyer gets a
bright idea. "*I'm* buying," he says. "I could take it
for him."

She looks at him with a reserved scowl—reserved for the money yet in his hand. "Is it *your* cambra?"

"No."

"Is the pitcher for you?"

"No."

"Well den." And they close the deal. The false buyer leaves, *uppity* in his mind. He considered buying something to get the picture, but the word "extortion" or some such got to him. He don't know she knew he wouldn't buy, she wasn't trying to sell anything, she was just stopping the picture-taking.

Well, that's what happens when a plain camera comes around. But when the federal oral boys rolled up looking like Fellini with zits and surrounded them with a TV studio—brushed aluminum and diffusion parasols—and scared them with the full brunt of the Modern Age, they took it, staring into the indigo zoom. Great big glass eye looking like a gasoline spill on a black tar road.

It makes me think of the *first* federal historians. What a time! The W.P.A. hired writers to write stuff like this. At least I have this book the Doctor said was very good and it seemed like this kind of stuff. But those writers were invisible, perched up in a corner watching sharecroppers bag z's, composing with a whispering pencil. Today's federal historians perch *you* up, light you up, make you up, and put you in the can, electronically. So here's the part of basket weaving that they got, which they wanted to get—Theenie and her aunt sit there weaving away. They wrap coils of grass around the shape in their mind and tie the coils in with other straw, which they push through with one tine of a fork. They mix in dark pine straw to make their design. They reach into their grocery bags for grass and keep building the coils. Their eyes never leave the work except when tourist money comes out of a pocket.

Then something happened, right in the middle of a perfectly good taping. The bag holding the green and brown spray of grass and pine needles fell and exposed Theenie's feet, and one of them was in a slipper, which was fine, and one of them was in a steaming half of a sweet potato, which was not fine.

"What is *that*?" cried the sociologist behind the camera.

Looking down at it, the other historian bent over and accidentally let the boom mike into the picture, like a closed umbrella pointing at the potato, going to stick it.

"Cut," said the first cameraman. "Dammit, it was perfect."

"We can edit it," said the sound man, and that's all you see, except for the sound man's head going in for a look at Theenie's foot in the potato, like he's going to hold his nose. His head is at the very bottom corner of the frame looking at it, and Theenie is in full center, looking at the camera with the face of a bull. Then they cut the filming.

"Never did edit out that damn potato," the pale one says when the show was over.

"Why would you want to?" Taurus says.

"Hey. Who would like be*lieve* it wasn't a joke or Monty Python or something? This is *oral history*."

Taurus looked evenly at the six screens whining

off with little *piss* noises coming out. "I guess so," he said.

"Thanks for showing us," I said. "We got to go. Dr. Manigault is very grateful. I'd seen it." I lied. "It was him that needed—" Taurus was out the door; I was going to give them an oral history spew they'd never edit out.

But he was already down the hall.

"Hey. Let's go get something to eat."

"Like what?"

"Potatoes."

He smiled. "What was that, anyway?"

"They use them for corns and bunions. Potatoes are the second great cure."

"And the first?"

"Ammonia."

"Ammonia?"

"Yeah, except not like you said it. Say it *ah-MON-ia* and it'll cure whatever it won't clean."

The only thing I remember about the rest of the day is the shirt I had on. It was my green-and-yellow. I tried to picture a new universe of potato wearing, who could and who couldn't. It was at the Grand. Preston and Jinx had on potatoes big as brogans, flared open at the ankles like construction workers'. The bitches came in in high-heeled spuds as trim as cigars. Jake had on a nondescript pair. I had on some saddle oxfords, warm ones. Then I saw the oral history boys trying theirs on, and every time they reached for them, red sparks hit their fingers like Dorothy's red shoes. They couldn't get their potatoes on. The Doctor had a pair at the foot of the wicker settee which she chose not to put on.

They were out of style. She just sat on her legs folded up under her and had a dreamy look. Then I took mine off and tried on everybody else's, like Goldilocks. Daddy's were in a drawer at his desk with his golf shoes. He could wear them, I thought, for a special occasion. Then Taurus showed up very inconspicuous. He was kneeling down, I thought looking at his. Then I saw he was polishing his potatoes. He was the only one taking care of them. He was using a big Kiwi hardwood brush and the skins were lightly steaming, and the brush stroking through the steam pulled it in slow clouds like a tug on the waterway in the early mornings.

❧ / **W**hen we got out of the oral history studio we went over to the market to see some real basket weaving. It was going on as usual —about five or six ladies on their metal cafeteria chairs (they must have got a deal, or they closed a school out in the country, or it burned, except chairs). They were all set up on the outside corners of the old slave-market longhouses, surrounded by their four hundred straw artifacts and sacks of new grass and straw at their feet, in the sunshine. Just inside, where all the flea market tables were, it was dark, with all kinds of van people selling jewelry and belt buckles and other things you can get in a pawnshop.

The van people came every weekend and sold this stuff like portable garage sales, stopping in on Friday night to hold their booth and early Saturday setting up, mostly in the middle of the market. At the upper end, where the auction block for the slaves had been, they filled the market in with boutiques painted in pastels. They have antiques there too, but these

are on consignment from the North, Daddy says.
They also have fancy restaurants that write what
they have to eat on a blackboard outside so you
know the food is as fresh as new chalk. They should
use one of those at school, to upgrade the image:
"Today we have a fresh, steamed hot dog, pork
beans, butter squash, Tuesday surprise cake, cold,
sweet milk. $.35."

Then down at the far end it's no boutiques or
even van people, but Negroes selling vegetables. I
mean they *sell* them—running up and shouting
down a neighbor's price and demanding you feel
their tomatoes. That end of the market is like it was
before the front end got boutique cuisine and tur-
quoise. It is just heavy green paint, open rafters,
dirty shale floor, tables, and vegetables. It was like
that all the way, before: bats in the rafters and
pigeons, paint heavy as metal falling loose, piss in
the corners, bums, and very dark—except at one or
two places there were these enclosures, like a barbershop or a hot-dog joint.

But those places weren't boutique-y. No one went
in them, and they were run by Negroes. Well, someone went in them, I guess. Daddy took me in one
of them once, we were just walking around. I remember now. It was a place about as big as a car,
a room behind swirled old glass in green wood
framing, and up against the glass were pressed all
these clothes. Inside, there were some on hangers
and on a table, but a lot were just piled up against
the windows. Daddy stopped and went in.

A Negro, invisible except for his white shirt, was
in there.

"Yezza."

"Need suspenders."

Nothing.

"How much are your suspenders?"

" 'Pend which."

Daddy plunged his hand into the wall of clothes at the door, and I saw through the window this banded strip of material with a brass buckle disappear into the dark mountain like a snake into the ground. The strip snapped free inside.

"These," he said, holding up a brown-and-white set of suspenders.

The Negro felt them and said a dollar. Daddy got them.

"Those would cost you fifteen dollars on King Street," he said, when we left. And suddenly we were looking into a barbershop, built like the haberdasher's, with another lone Negro very much like the first, but this one behind a barber chair with white porcelain armrests and a white porcelain headrest, looking twenty degrees away from us.

Then there was this food place where you stepped up to a half-open door and ordered.

"I'm hungry."

"All right, let's go on up to Hen—" He stopped. "What do you want to eat?"

"What do they have here?"

"Let's see."

We did, and had two very reasonable hot dogs and Pepsis in Coke cups—they explained the difference before they sold them to us. They put ice cubes from an ice-cube tray in them out of a refrigerator like at a house.

The next time I went to the market it was all gone. Bats, rafters, shale, pee, lead paint, clothes wads, the stuck barber pole, chili in open pots, all went to dropped ceilings for energy saving, parquet, restrooms, pastel, jean shops, international flags waving in front of a deli store, and food described on a blackboard. It was something.

The only thing left intact was the vegetable end, where, besides the women shouting could they help us with something that day, Daddy and I saw this kid with a big dog on a kite string leash.

He was going from table to table piled high with vegetables, showing it off. "Lookit my new collie!" They couldn't help but lookit: it was tall as his shoulders, and prancing ahead of him without straining the kite string, as if it had been trained. Its back was bowed up and it had a long, skinny bone-head, and the whole dog was about half a foot wide, like it was sick, and smiling.

"What's wrong with that dog?"

"Probably nothing," Daddy said. "Except he's lost."

"Lost from where?"

"From his owner."

"It's not his Bonsai?"

"That's a Borzoi."

That's where I learned they weren't Bonsais, but they still look as tortured as those little trees they plant in square china pots. Daddy made a call from the corner and a big car came around in a minute and Daddy told the man to go up the market.

"On a *string*?" the man said, laughing. "They something *else*, aindee, Iv?" He sped off.

Daddy's name is Everson Simons Manigault. You

shorten names here to the least sound workable and then, if you can, change the sound. *Iv.* A regal name like Cambridge becomes *Bridge*, then *Brudge*, then *Budge*. And so forth. Girls, sometimes it's lengthened. Mary can't be plain Mary, but Mary C., stuck on. Anne won't do, it becomes Annie, still something missing, so Annie-*boo*. People get more charming that way, more memorable and distinct.

"Who was that man?" I asked Daddy.

"Old friend of mine from Clemson," he said.

"What's his name?"

"Bun."

We Entertain: A Faculty Raree

❧   /   Something more than all get-out. That was the phrase at school one year. Sharp as all get-out. Fast as all get-out. Where did it come from? What could it mean? Well, the night the Doctor had her associates over to inspect her circus property, it was ludicrous as all get-out.

I had to get the party condiments out of the Cadillac. She'd got a bunch of things she never drank herself, like Wild Turkey and J&B Scotch, to impress the guests with. And a box of Coke and things for mixing it. It was quite a load, though at the time I didn't notice, except for the insane trips with one bottle in each hand so I wouldn't break anything like I did once. "Please, honey, no more than two at a time. I don't want you to strain." She was always referring to the time a blue crab scared me on the steps and I bailed out because I was still in my childhood mode. He was perfectly crushed and pickled by the best discount liquor money could buy when she got there, holding the door open,

looking down truly aghast, the lame crab waving
his last threats from a pile of glass and wet paper
sacking and sharp whiskey stink. She replaced everything with one stop at the Grand bootleg door, the
day I first heard her called the Duchess, and the day
they first saw her little prince. Apparently I did
something to impress them, like pet a bad dog or
look in its ears and tell them it had mice, which I
thought was plural for "mite" then. We went home
and transferred the cheap stuff to her decanters and
got ready for *that* party.

And ever since I have been a two-bottle lackey.
Tonight was big if you considered the number of my
trips. And on one of them I met her coming down
with a coat on her shoulders, and she went up the
beach toward Theenie's. I thought she meant to get
Theenie for a vacuum run, or even for maid work
during the bash, until I remembered Theenie was
gone. She was up there to talk to the star boarder.
I was so dense, picturing him cracking ice for them
or driving the soddy ones home. He was going to
be *it*, guest of honor.

The party collects very quickly because it is so
casual, twos and singles parking up the road in the
palmettos, which they think of as the jungle, and
they walk in like soldiers on leave from all their
trench work teaching their *ignorami*, which great
parts of their conversation dwell on in the early
going. No one can write or read or—brace yourself—
think in any of my classes. Nor mine. Nods. Toasts.
A few more rounds and the culprit has been de-
termined: the president of the college! Not the

dean, not social promotions, not even their less adept colleagues (everyone not present). It's the president. Then president stories.

The president was a general in the army before he was a college president, which allowed him to view academic developments in martial terms. So funds were not appropriated by budgetary solicitation, the till was sacked. The fine-arts department was not enlarged, it was reinforced. So-and-So would not be denied tenure, he would be discharged without dishonor. They called him the General.

"The General went up to poor Bill," somebody says, "and smiled so effusively Bill thinks he's in trouble. Then he said he'd heard Bill planned to get married." They howled, because Bill knows the General knows he's homo. He's so scared for his job he can't teach!

But the way the General most significantly ruined the school was by designating department heads from the outside, rather than by promoting from within. This not only leaves them all unpromoted but at one time eight department heads were from military colleges or West Point itself, and the faculty meetings "sounded like Yalta," somebody said. "*Enfilades*, for Christ's sake. I need smaller sophomore sections and he says to me, in public, if I can't run a full company, fall to the rear."

"Get off the pot," somebody seconds, the party beginning to roll. But they never get very far with the General, because the campaign he runs is successful. They just don't like the language. And he's so powerful that even their most inept colleagues are reprieved and warmly taken back, because their fragile roles in the total ruination of education are by comparison so minor and incidental.

But after a time gossip beats out professional problems, and all gossip is finally about sex and a lot of giggling gets going, with grown men putting their heads between their own knees and laughing at the floor about, say, a wager someone present has made that someone absent always takes a shower after "doing it." "Whenever she'll let him." "Whenever he'll let *her*!" Red faces buried in the bouncing knees, people going to the sideboard and losing count—something they rarely do. These are drink accountants.

Well, it's one of these when Taurus drops in and hurls the talk backward through sexual indiscretion and the faults of the president and the failure of mind in America to a *real* problem: How to accommodate a nonprofessional guest who is not a servant or a child or an old friend of the hostess? Play it by ear, play it by ear.

Well, he knows his moves, I see. Goes to the sideboard and's got a decanter top off and decanter on tilt when he sees no glass, only the Doctor's metal Depression tumblers, which make stuff taste like water squeezed out of electrical cord. He turns and gives me a high sign (I'm in the kitchen see-through) to bring him a glass. I carry it out like I was just going that way anyway, and he pours into it, still in my hand, sets the decanter back, and turns and takes the drink after he's surveyed the whole room. They are studying other things, in other directions than his, to a man. So I know and he knows, I see him smiling. It's the first time since Theenie took off

like all get-out that I've really considered the large
public questions about him and the situation. Like
who is he? What's he doing here?

Before I even get out of the way, a woman of
whom it's rumored her husband was found in a
motel room with another man on the faculty comes
up and puts her hand on his arm and says, "We've
heard quite a bit about you, young man." That's a
title I get a lot during these parties, but tonight it's
his and it's different. It sounds more suspicious on
him because he *is* one. I guess about twenty-five.
Maybe thirty.

"I'm Margaret Pinckney," she says to him, ad-
justing her arm on his. "I'd introduce you to my
husband, Jim, but he's not here." Jim's the one they
said was in the motel. She's dressed up more than
any other woman there.

"Well, Mahhgret, I see you've *met* him." It's the
Bill they howled about in the president story, flutter-
ing his eyelids and blushing—won't look at either
Margaret or Taurus, but holds out his hand, without
saying his name, to Taurus, who shakes it. Then, I
guess before they could regroup, Taurus cruises off
toward the Doctor, who is entertaining.

"Bill, isn't *Jim* enough?" says Margaret.

"Enough whaat, Mahhgret?"

"Enough you *know* what."

Bill blushed. "Mahhgret, you don't understayan—"

"Yes, I do," she says, turning from the sideboard
with a whole tumbler of bourbon. "I understand
perfectly that you people can't just be per*ni*cious.
You've got to be pro*mis*cuous on top of that." I hide,
more or less, under the sideboard.

"Mahhgret, now who is *we*? And anyway, *we* didn't do anything to Jim, honey. Why that tendency's been *quite* around, quite some—"

"*Schmendency*! It's cannibalism, human larceny! And you've got to come over here just now when I'm talking to Dr. Manny's new—"

"New *what*, Mahhgret?"

"Her new friend."

"Free-yend. Look at that bohunk. *I* heard he's her second *thesis*, honey."

This one confused me at the time, made me suddenly self-conscious, crouching like a halfback, in full view under the sideboard, so I trotted off to the kitchen, kind of burning somewhere, almost wishing I had for cover a broom horse between my legs. But I saw Margaret Pinckney leaving the area, too —at an angle, but holding her tall tumbler at plumb, letting it lead her. I think she took all the attention.

You can't retreat to your room during one of these deals, because browsers stroll in and look at the book titles and try to talk to you, and the telescope trick I worked on the coroner won't hold up all night—in fact, it will draw more of these professional people in. So I went down to Theenie's to read W.P.A. stories.

For a long time I thought that the Negro who papered those walls just did it random from a pile of newspapers on his worktable in the center of the room, and there were so many W.P.A. stories in the papers of 1937 that he just slapped up story after story or page after page and they were all accidentally on the W.P.A. Right next to a full feature

on the Fair Park they built in Dallas, with all that
heavy extra stone, was an account of how many
new ditches were dug in Montgomery, which was
going to be bad news for mosquitoes, and next to
that how many writers had been assigned to make
new plays for the stone-heavy theater that was going
up, etc. And one day it came to me: the paperhanger
had to select the stories out. There had to be bread-
line stories before there were W.P.A. stories, and
stock-market stories before that. So a Negro with
scissors in that shack so new it had good fresh
black tar paper on the outside goes through a ton of
newspapers and pulls out the stories he likes, a man
with no job clipping out all these manufactured jobs
he couldn't even get to or probably land if he did get
to, with a bucket of flour and water and a stick to
stir with and his hand to wipe it on and lay in the
wonderful stories. They were good enough stories
on their own, but when I figured out this new aspect,
they got better. Somehow, standing on Theenie's
bed or on a chair reading them, I was closer to what
really happened, if not to how it was to hold a
made-up job, then how it was to hold in reverence
their making up. It was a swell, poor time, I know.

There was always a new story to read, it seems,
or even if you thought you had read one before, a
new way to imagine the Negro reading it first, and
so it became a new kind of story. Or maybe he
couldn't even read. Maybe he could just detect
W.P.A. and cut out the connected columns, knowing
or trusting it was the good stuff. Maybe he was
even not in gloried awe of the Project, didn't even

know what it was. He could have thought W.P.A. was for "White People's Advantages" or something. Maybe he was bitter and political in that shack in 1937. Who knows?

But anyway, you could always read and reread, changing your opinion about the Negro and so changing the stories and their effect now. I read them that night until Taurus showed back up.

"Is it over?"

"Near enough."

"You want to do something tomorrow?"

"Yeah. Come get me—*after* cartoons."

Cartoons. Consummate comedian he was. I went back to the house and slipped in and it wasn't over. It was blumberville. Infamous motel Jim Pinckney had just got there.

"Well, what's this guy like?" he said.

"Her second *thesis*?" Bill giggled.

"Or her second honeym—" Margaret was slurry and too slow.

"I don't believe a word of it," Bill said. "Not a word. A Neeegrow. He's as much black as I am."

Everybody looked at Bill, who blushed.

"A *Nee*-grow!" Jim said. "Jesus Christ." Jim was Old Guard.

"So she sayez," Bill put in. "Moreover, sired by a famous writer."

"Of the school—the Famous Writers School? 'Sired by Famous Writer out of Negress—'"

"Shut up, Jim," said the Doctor, who on her folded-up legs was weaving slightly in the wicker settee.

"Yesss, honey. *Do*," said Margaret, who was patting

the Doctor. "*Some* of us still have regular *hopes* in this world."

Peals and knee-bouncing by Bill and Jim, Bill looking at the ceiling finally, with tears in his eyes.

I slipped outside and went up the front stairs and climbed in the window to my room and didn't hear any more of it. But this is where I learned all the crap on him they had, and, I thought, the main reason she was hyped up on him. If she even *thought* his father was a writer, then he was supposed to influence, any way it might happen, me.

On the Prevention of —ease Only

☙ / For a while there I guess he was still serving papers out of Charleston, because I would ride the bus home like always, except of course for the rear-door positioning. He dropped me off in the morning and went on up and got some blue folders with the criminal activities alleged therein and fell to on the people while I was in school. He said it was kind of hard, doing it, not being the law but just a kind of citizen-scab, a bounty hunter for gunslingers so small that they didn't spend tax money on the sheriff to go get them with. They weren't gunslingers, though— bad-check slingers, bad-language slingers. Mostly the baddest thing they committed, he said, was bad judgment. He didn't like it and said sometimes he let the people go. All that does is delay things. The paper reverts to the attorney's office and doesn't look too good on his service record, and he said his attorneys knew from the cases he *had* found that there was something fishy when he gave up and turned one back in.

So he's out being Matt Dillon, chasing down rotten-teeth van people and gold-teeth Negroes descendent of Oglethorpe convicts and slaves, and I'm in the front seat of the bus like a bus rider emeritus. For a while there were jokes. "Hey, Sim! Comone back heah. The *air* better." At home the sun would be swung around and low, about ten feet up in the air. Its angle was perfect for about two hours to fill up the house with mirror light glaring up off the ocean, blinding upward through the sliding doors onto the ceiling so that any shadows thrown were thrown out the windows and you never saw them. It made it like a dollhouse or a perfectly lit stage set. The wind kept whistling that peppery noise against the house, little sand grains working their way through some-how, tumbling in their little glassy bounce across the floors like an eminent-domain march to the other side of the room, and piling up on false Edens such as a throw rug or under the TV. So I'm in there looking at the flash of ocean, moved by the heat in the direction of the sand, shadowless and hot, quiet except for the peppering which you quit hearing, wondering about things, touching the wicker to make it squeak, the glass decanters and their little tin bibs on chains telling you what kind of poison they hold, feeling the drapes, which lift off the floor like old big rats are behind every one of them, listening for a clue about something I can't even figure out what it's about.

And nothing happens. At a time like this you

expect some news, an event, maybe just some excite-
ment. But it doesn't come. The sun swings on
around and throws the set into the cool, dusky after-
time of the studio or stage where everything had been
ready, lights and camera and player and no one to
clap together two striped barricades and simply yell,
Action. Instead, the lights quit and quiet and cool;
dim dusk dawns on the regular old house, the plain
land sales office pagoda.

"Sim!" Theenie would say if she caught me in
one of these conditions. "What ails *you*?"

"Nothing."

"Somethin' ailin' you."

"Nothing."

"Hmmp!" she would say, going about her business.

Or I could take the talkative route: "Nothing ever
happens, Theenie."

"Say whah?" Very high.

"I said, *Nothing ever happens*."

"Hmmp!" she would say, going about her business.

One time I said: "I'm worried, Theenie."

"What *choo* worrit about." Not a question, a denial
of my right or cause to worry, against the larger
monopoly of adult rights.

"Puberty." I looked at her to see if it worked. She
looked like a horse in a stall wondering whether to
kick a careless stable boy, eyes orbiting in quick
white slices like quarter moons.

"I'm worried about this thing they call puberty."

"You *scudgin'* me. Why you wont to grind me,
Sim?" and she flopped all the ironing together, which
would have otherwise taken a half hour to fold up,

and left, silent until tomorrow, until a short trial during which I could not refer to the question would secure my reprieve, and we could be jake again. If I did it like that, a puberty question was just a souvenir in the memory of her raising me up, but if I asked again, I was closer to a hellion. She could tell people how sweet I was to have asked, but not that she had to answer. It's *part* race relations and part family relations, there.

So there in the upward glare of clinical Atlantic radiation I remain—before the Doctor comes in with a batch of papers to grade, new bottle in a skintight paper sack twisted around the neck. The breaking seal will suck a little air out of the kitchen, like the hiccup of a baby, air that slips into the bottle and hits the liquor and changes it like film or blood: blood, film, liquor are never seen before their innocence is lost. Also in this air-innocence class is rubbers, which didn't get into the class for a while because I didn't know what they were. In the top drawer of the Progenitor's chest I found these gold-coin-like deals almost like candy mints except, thank God, light enough to tip me off before I tried to eat one. Then I thought they were amusement-park tokens or pirate doubloons you buy drinks with in a resort-town bar or something. Then I figured they were gambling chips from the Bahamas, where they'd been on a trip. Gambling chips—I was close.

Anyway, the matter came up at school and somehow I learned what they were for, if not exactly what they were, so in one of our first Big Brother reunions after the Progenitor left, I advanced the line of inquiry about rubbers. "They stop babies, okay, I got that much, but *how*?"

"Well," he said, "you put them on."

"How?"

"Well—" He fumbled in the air in front of the steering wheel; we were in his car, engine running. He tucked the fingers on one hand into the palm of the other. Suddenly he rested his hands. "Like a sock."

"Like a *sock*?"

"Yessir," he said, nodding, and very satisfied about something. "Anything *else* you want to know?" Else?

"No, sir."

"Sure?"

"Yes, sir." He left out the *juice* part, the good part, left me imagining your tallywhacker (the Doctor's favorite word for it) is some kind of electric eel or polyp stinger you have to insulate with rubber. Nothing about it stopping the paste of life. I have to learn about that at the back of the bus, where you can learn all you need to know on earth. *Brylcreem*, they said, and *feels good*. So. A *sock* stops hairdressing. One of the big disappointments of my childhood, I tell you.

But I had this talk with Taurus in the early days, just to check him out further with the Boy Act.

"I'm worried."

He was carefully matching the thread lines of the bottle to the lip of a drinking jar, and he poured a thin sheet of whiskey into the jar, just covering the bottom. It was snifter drinking without crystal or brandy. He swirled it more than he drank it. In

Theenie's cabin it still smelled like a washed dog sometimes. His nose hovered over the amber film in the glass.

"Okay," he said. He was not the target that Theenie was.

"I'm worried about puberty."

He smiled. "Don't."

"Why not?"

"It's too big."

"What do you mean?"

"Like nuclear war. Nothing to worry about."

"It comes or it doesn't?"

"Yes. Except here, it's coming. So there's less to worry about than nuclear war."

"There's a lot of bad information floating around," I said.

"You'll get through."

"My father told me a rubber was like a *sock*."

He pushed his lips together over the jar. "Well, what's wrong with that?"

I stopped. He was scudgin' *me*. "Well—because it's more like a *balloon*, if anything," I said, hoping I was right.

"Sock, balloon," he said, in that kind of Jewish resigning whine they do on TV. "When the time comes, you won't blow it up, you won't put it on your foot." He looked at me. "I hope."

"So there's *nothing* to worry about?"

He got up and prepared me one of these poverty snifters and pushed it over the enamel table and sat back down.

"Worry about this. You will need a girl. The sooner it hits, the better."

"It hits?"

"Well, no. It creeps up."

"Your sac gets ruddy like a bum's nose," I said.

"Where'd you hear that?"

"I *saw* it. We got this guy down at the Y who wouldn't take off his bathing suit because he said he was older and it took about three hundred of us, heads walloping banging lockers, but we did it."

"And his equipment looked like a *bum's* nose?"

"Well, no. But it was—I under*stand* it gets bigger —but it was dark and more wrinkly. Like whiskey drinkers' faces if they're really gone."

"I see." He snifted. "Well, after your bum's nose comes in, you will need a girl. This is the only thing to worry about. They will tell you you don't need one and they will tell the girls the same thing, so it can take longer to find one than it should."

He fixed me another volume-less drink, and him too.

"So do this. There's a kind of girl who won't listen to them, and you need to study them. How old are you?"

"Twelve."

He smiled. "Are there any special girls you know?"

"Diane Parker takes her clothes off for a quarter. But I never went with them to see it. And a girl named Andrea gave us the lowdown on the girls' movie last year, and a pamphlet they gave them about beginning to bleed. God, that's creepy—"

"Okay. Not these girls themselves necessarily, but see if you can get a line on their character traits and what they're like generally. Get to know them. Find one with some brains when the time comes and use a balloon or use her ideas if she has any."

I considered this. We must have looked like a real couple of cards, an ace and a joker maybe, sitting there in a haint-painted shack on a whistling bluff on the nowhere coast of Edisto, itself a speck on the Atlantic seaboard.

"At the Grand," I said, "one of the rubber machines says *Sold for prevention of —ease only*. What does the scratched-out *—ease* mean?"

"You'll get the joke in time," he said. "It was *disease* originally. Don't worry about that either. It comes or it doesn't. Probably does. Don't get anybody pregnant is the other thing. When the time comes, if you don't know what that means, *find out*."

"Girls get *boys* in trouble, you mean?"

He said yes and smiled, and I don't think knew whether I was joking or not, but didn't need to know. That's the thing I learned from him during those days: you can wait to know something like waiting for a dream to surface in the morning, which if you jump up and wonder hard you will never remember, but if you just lie there and listen to the suck-pump chop of the surf and the peppering and the palm thrashing and feel the rising glare of Atlantic heat, you can remember all the things of the night. But if you go around beating the world with questions like a reporter or federal oral history junior sociologist number-two pencil electronic keyout asshole, all the answers will go back into mystery like fiddlers into pluff mud. You just sit down in the marsh and watch mystery peek out and begin to nibble the air and saw and sing and run from hole to hole with itself. Lie down and the fiddlers will come as close to you as trained squirrels in a park. And how did he teach me that? I don't know, but you don't need a package of peanuts or anything.

A New Kind of Custody Junket Dawns

❧ / About this time began a run of events. The first one was so weird that I remember what shirt I was wearing. It was Friday, and I came home on the bus (Taurus was out serving, I guess) and had run up the steps before I saw both the Doctor's and the Progenitor's cars, his a little crooked in the driveway. It was one of those deals where you become an eavesdropper accidentally and have to pick your moment to declare yourself so they won't know what you heard, or at least will think you didn't hear the worst of it. Through the screen I could make out their silhouettes like in a TV interview of double agents or criminals or state witnesses where they backlight and underexpose to protect the identity of the guilty and sometimes they even woof out voices so they sound like speech-therapy patients or retards or robots.

"The hell I can't," I heard him say.

"Everson. I still don't see what you're so worked—"

"What's so difficult? Every veterinarian with an

autopsy license is one thing, but I can go a lot further with—with your bounty hunter."

"You're a *son* of a *bitch*." She snapped it hard.

"I will take him."

"No, you won't. You can't."

"The hell I can't."

I figured I had the beat, so I stepped three steps down from where my lips had been pressing on the rusty, fly-smelling screen and stomped back up and sashayed in with a perfect whine-bang door slam and was on them so fast they never knew or suspected. Looked like big doings: she didn't have a drink, he did.

"Hi, Daddy." We did the hug. "Am I late or you early?"

"I'm early," he said, and looked at the Doctor. "And late."

"We still going?" I asked.

"Sure—why not?"

"Don't know," I said, going to my room for my tote bag. It was highly unusual for him to come inside the house like this to get me. The shirt I had on was my red Rugby.

That weekend was the second event. We usually did everything as if it was the state fair. It was like he took me out to show me a good time and I could play games or ride rides if I wanted to, except it was movies and restaurants we went to. But this time we went over to a woman's house I only later put together was his secretary but then instead got the idea a lawyer herself. She had this kid about two years older than me, and they put us together to entertain ourselves while they sat and talked. She lived in a carriage house and they had the whole yard of the big house, which looked empty.

Sometimes kids just hit it off despite the artificial confinement, which is strange. Fully aware of the difficulty of liking each other, like in an arranged marriage, we just put all that aside and had a blast. I don't know how it started but Mike, her kid, said that we could ride his go-cart if we put on the new wheel and didn't go in the street. The new wheel was wrapped in brown paper and was in a closet full of his mother's shoes and when he went in to get it he had to walk on the shoes and he fell over. Well, the wheel was heavy and he couldn't pick it up lying there, so he tried to get up and the shoes kept buckling and sliding and turning his ankles and we started laughing.

"Here. Roll it to me."

We rolled it out over the crumbly terrain—all these Italian high-heeled shoes and boots as soft as puppies—and we couldn't stop laughing. Anyway, we got the wheel out and put it on the go-cart, re-using the cotter pin, and fired the engine up. Mike called it the cocker pin. He had this track charted out through little places where you could hardly make it, and every time one of us hit a banana tree it was funnier than the shoes. You just get laughing and can't stop.

We ran the course until white roots were showing in the mud at the turns and the engine smoked and ticked out a blue vapor. Then we went in and Mike, who had got the idea I was smart because I said we

could use a nail if straightening out that cotter pin
was too hard, showed me this kind of altar in his
room. It was his books, about ten books and some
magazines like *National Geographic*. He told me he
was through with comics. Over the books on a small
banner he had written:

MY GOAL IN LIFE: NOT TO BE A IGNORAMUS
THATS MY MOTO

He showed me this shrine very proudly.

"That's a good motto," I said. I didn't know what
to do about the spelling, so I didn't do anything.

The important thing, I suppose, is that this weekend was the first one we spent that wasn't entirely
at the state fair or big-brother Disneyland. It was
the first time Daddy sort of ignored me like the
Doctor, and I must confess that I had a better time
than ever before on these custody junkets. It's heavy
pressure, you know, to find your role four days out
of the month, a little two-day run every two weeks
with no rehearsal. I suppose it was no fun for him,
either, being the director as well as actor and still
not getting it right. But that weekend he seemed a
lot more regular in a way it's hard to describe. I
think that woman (Mike's mother) looked sexy, for
one thing, but that is strictly my unhaired opinion.
At school the word is, you don't know what girls
really are until you have hair, kind of a Samson
thing, I guess. I regularly enjoy unveiling mythic
structure in Bluffton Elementary education. Taurus
knows, I am pretty sure, from this exchange I wit-

nessed between him and a girl who served us in a restaurant, but I am still sorting that out and finishing it.

On Monday morning early, when I got back, there was fog in the palmettos and the tree edges looked blue. Taurus's car was parked and spiffing out white balls of smoke into the fog, like smoke rings. Daddy stopped the car with the shift stick and it clicked to a stop like the ratchet stands I got to help set up for the drums one night at the Baby Grand for this old drummer with a band that had been everywhere. It was the saxophone player that was famous, and the rest of the band was nobody, so they had to do all the work. The drummer let me open out these chrome stands that had silver feet and arms you stood up and set the right-size drum in. He did that part. The stands clicked until they were open and then wouldn't close. The drum heads were worn clean in the centers but had this crud all around the edge you could scrape off with your fingernail, like a crayon deal where you color all the colors on the paper and then black all over that and then etch a design by scraping off the black, leaving a rainbow-y picture. On the drum this left a pure-white scratch mark.

Anyway, he stopped the car like a ratchet stand and was up the stairs before I had the tote bag out of the back seat, and I thought he was going in, but he stopped. He turned and waited for me on the landing and said goodbye and left. That was very strange—getting out, for one thing, and then going up there and *not* going in but turning and seeing me up like a guest, and then our doing the hug and him leaving. They were waiting inside as I crossed the unswept floor. I noticed all the windows were open and the drapes standing out like air-conditioner sales strips. You couldn't see it but you could feel the damp clam of fog on everything. The Doctor was in her wicker pose and the settee was cricking crisply in the cool air and they both had these steaming black coffees and were looking patiently at each other.

"Hi, Ducks," she said.

"Hi."

"Everything okay?"

"Just fine."

"Ready for school?"

I was in my room and stopped. "Ready as ever," I said. Apparently it was another shirt day, so I got a black Western rig with bat-wing shoulders, makes me look like Wyatt Earp.

When I came out Taurus was saying, "It sounds queer to me."

"Well," she said, sipping coffee to punctuate as for a lecture point. "What have you seen out here that wasn't?"

"Well," he said, doing the same coffee thing, "aren't you divorced?"

"We can still be friends, then?" She hurried on, ignoring him.

He tipped his cup at her. "Why not?"

"I mean . . ."

"Sport," he said to me, "let's go." We were off, me to school to drive fat pencils into newsprint, him to Charleston to catch crooks too cheap for the government to bother.

The End of Inquiry by Direct Methods

❧ / It looked about time I did some investigation of girls. Diane Parker was still a quarter, so I got in on one of these field trips. It was very subtle.

Diane got her quarters from five of us, and we all left the bus-stop zone together at a trot and went into the woods. School woods always have a greasy worn-out feel from regular and undeviating use by kids. You always see a rubber or a rubber package, but more distinctive is this special compound of sand and pine straw which makes pine straw look dirty for the only time in its life, packed around the edges of deep trails like base-running paths on the playground.

Well, on this gunky straw Diane pulled her pants down and we looked for about five seconds. Then she was headed back up the trail fast, leaving us with the mystery. Before we could begin to work on it, we saw the bus and started running too—again very subtle, all of us running after Diane Parker out of the woods. She made $1.25. I had this feeling sort of like I needed to pee when I saw her naked. This was aggravated during the run to the bus, but subsided. I could find out what this was if I pored over the literature, but I frankly don't care to. I am sure that Diane met her contractual obligations, showing us what she did, but I knew when I saw it that there was more to it than this little cleft-chin thing you marvel at how smooth it looks. I thought at least it would move. Which speaks my case: all the hollering about this soft little nose you can see for a quarter is about something else. What, I don't know.

Well, from here you have two paths of inquiry. It's like you've seen the text and now you can consult the critics or the artist. The Doctor showed me this stuff. We have all these critical editions with your essays and writer interviews right in them. I had seen the text for five seconds, so I got an eighth-grade critic. "Of course you get inside it, fotch," says one celebrated pundit for my barbecued Fritos. "Well, what's it like?" I say, not even sure I mean to ask what it *feels* like. "It's not *like* anything," he says. "You just have to do it yourself." I suspect he hasn't "done it."

At this point benevolence steps up, and for no more of my lunch I am awarded this news by Roland, the patrol boy who jumped out of the bus, they said, the time I fell out, and was the first one to the tree where I stopped rolling. "It's like in your mouth. Feel in your cheek," he says, distending his cheek with his finger inside his mouth. I do this. *"Yeah,"* says the first guy with my Fritos. "It's *sorta* like that."

Well, swell. I now know a whole hell of a lot more than I did. So I will have to go back to the source. To hell with the critics.

Now, your artists are somewhat famous, I gather, for playing around with people who ask them what it all means, which is why one interview spawns more critical essays than the book ever did. So I had to be careful. But then how careful can you be, asking a girl under fifteen something like this? So I shoot the moon, as it were, because there's this girl who disappeared last year—some said to have a baby and some said to go to reform school and some said both—but anyway, she looked very adult coming back, always had a purse with her and a sweater on her shoulders like a cape. And she got a lot of attention from back-of-the-room types, which she largely ignored, except it made her hold her head and walk different going away from them.

Well, it's bold because against her league I look like Spanky McFarland trying to have a word with Marlene Dietrich. In fact, I chicken out altogether. I can't even phrase anything for a foot in the door. But fortune of fortunes, she gets on our bus one day, heads right to the back, and holds court. Now this is entirely another class of thing than a Diane Parker selling peeks. You get the idea she would think that kind of thing cheap or childish.

When I get back there to sidle in, the guys are saying she should get off at their stops or come home to play cards or something, saying it very smoothly.

"I'm not playing no strip poker with *you* guys," she says. The *you* creates an image of *other* guys.

How did she know they meant strip poker? That's what they're all trying to figure out, I think, when she seizes their indecision and delivers a wallop worthy of a woman who has had a baby out of wedlock in a state reform school.

"Do you guys know what it's like to eat a woman?"

They don't. They all get these strong, silent looks on their faces except one, who smiles. He figures, I think, that this is so far beyond the pale, so far beyond, say, getting a long look at things in a poker game that they don't even have to pretend to know. So he says very candidly and calmly, "No, we don't." And then, "So tell us what it's like."

She thinks a minute, purse on her shoulder, and says like Miss Kitty on *Gunsmoke* would say to a table of ruffians before Matt got back: "It's like sucking mayonnaise through a Brillo pad."

This had quite an effect on the ruffians. On me, too. My investigations had gone far enough for the time being. I stopped this kind of questioning forever, and had a strange kind of respect for that girl, and still do.

A *Time Like Sweet Potatoes*

❧ / There's been one positive positive about all this going-to-be-a-writer bull-hockey, and that is what our most famous playwright helped me get away with. Researching Habits and Methods for me the Doctor discovers that he gets up at three o'clock and makes coffee and plays rock and roll and writes, *still* writes plays. Well, a master sets a precedent and it is available for all the trials of posterity. And I am posterity.

It gets outlawed on school nights is the only thing. And I modify two ingredients at least. Three a.m. is perfect—he got that right. The house is kind of horror-movie still, settling itself for the night yet, and the wicker furniture is silently crisp; the Doctor is retired from the labors of lion's Kool-Aid and snoring on her side when I pull her door shut. Wind is whistling the sand, and surf chomping like a roaring crowd, but it is somehow very quiet all the same.

Coffee I change to this recipe: I put just enough instant coffee in to give an adult look to milk and drink that. I think it's the smell of coffee people like anyway, which you get, this way.

And rock and roll. A big thing has happened there. The dramatist meant something like Elvis Presley or Jerry Lee Lewis on those Tennessee Sun records when it was really black music in white hands or something—he can't mean The Strawberry Alarm Clock. Old Presley the truck jockey in his leather jacket and natural sneer violating teenage girls within range of his voice—something like that helps him write. Not "Time" poems by a spoken voice in a group called The Moody Blues. Maybe the closest thing going to what he meant was this Jim Morrison cat, who a very correct know-it-all at school with all these appointments to play his clarinet at ladies' parties told us was arrested in Miami for "masticating" on stage.

"Tobacco?" I said.

"*No-*o. *Mas*ticating," he said, like I was a dunce. Well, I was and I wasn't, because if you look it up, "chewing" is about as close to meaning something as "manipulating." And when you've had one of these mayonnaise questionnaires backfire on you, masticating will suffice. So I have no real idea what Morrison did, even though I know the *word*, but anyway, he's dead.

So I skip it, the rock and roll, and tune in one of these weather-farm-fishing shows where the guy sounds like a very young grandfather, and in two hours you know whether to cut tobacco or go fishing or stay in bed, and you have this cozy feeling because a grandfather like that is free, and useful to all of us. He talks about Russians and crime and rain, and his voice never changes. Someone calls in that 139 Soviet spies are registered in D.C. and the F.B.I. does nothing about it, and someone else calls and says 139 channel bass were landed at Botany Bay, and it's still 5:35 a.m. in WQUE country, and Pop's very charming and full-sounding. It's probably some skinny guy with a big Adam's apple and bad skin, but he sure sounds like a green-and-black mackinaw and a pipe.

My other modification is a hamburger. I don't know what it is, but I make a hamburger all the way, and down it and get wired. You have to fry it hard to get this chewy black crust on it, and singe the bread in the pan too, and heavy onions and mustard, and this at three-thirty in the morning is different than at any other time—it really gets me. All this, the farm news and the burger and the fake coffee, isolates you, but it ratifies you too, so that for a while I am lord of the manor, looking up and down the coast as if I were proprietor of the Atlantic herself or governor of all rumrunners. This is also when I write stuff. (Or used to. I've about quit all the other crap except this assignment.)

The 3 a.m. time is kind of like potatoes for corns on your feet—not for everybody. You can imagine who could do it and who couldn't conceive it. Now the Doctor couldn't personally, but it has its writerly vocational recommendations, so she lets me, but even she doesn't realize the regimen it's got to, the ritual of it. And if Daddy were here, I am sure it would be sufficient cause for another round at the pedi-shrink, where they took me because they thought I was retarded.

They did this little number with my knees and a hammer to make me think it was a regular visit and pumped up that armband job, which I thought was to test my muscle. Well, I bought it. So when the doctor says, "Simons," very slowly, "I want you to tell me what a few things are," I said okay.

"What's an envelope?" he asked.

"It's a thing you eat for breakfast," I popped.

This queer color went through everybody's face like heat lightning, and I knew something was wrong. So I thought, in the way you can if you're three years old and they're scudgin' you, very hard about my answer and the question, and it didn't fit right, not quite, even though I thought they should have given me some points for speed. Very sharply I slapped my forehead and said, "What am I doing, failing!"

And that reversed the heat lightning, calmed the waters of worry. No kid, master of the Boy Act at three, could, they figure, be retarded. So I was off. But it left an imprint. They didn't trust me. I knew. Nor I them.

I found out later it was the Doctor took me there, not the Progenitor. He thought I was regular for three, but she had to see if I could *ever* learn to read. Well, it's true I couldn't tie a shoe or stop wetting the bed, but those Golden Books never gave me a problem. And then it was on to all these award children's books about contemplative rabbits, and llamas that talk and go both ways, which I didn't know at the time was preparing me for faculty parties.

And then it was on to the Library itself, my book-walled bassinet, and the great stuff. Now, some of it's pretty good, but I spent a lot of misdirected energy being disappointed by titles, like I told you, things like *The Screwtape Letters*, which I thought was a transcript of tapes about you-know-whatting.

Anyway, smelling the coast in that gently howling pagoda at 3 a.m. got me to thinking about things that were going on. In a way, the house would tell me how to study things. The surf said more at a distance than up close. I was governor of the rum-runners inside the house, at a remove from the action, but outside I was a kid getting wet from the spray of the waves. Still, it seemed that things were happening, but when I looked squarely at them, I wasn't sure.

Like I get to tear up the yard of a big house and notice this kid's mother's bazongas and suddenly my father is a new beast for it—that's no event. And the faculty party is not exactly headlines—not even with me crouching under the sideboard to listen to the lushes and all of a sudden wondering about Taurus and the questions on the lushes' minds— that is not finally an event either, but it seemed so. Well, things like this piled up on me, little nothings that seemed like somethings.

One night in the playwright's patented ozone, watching the wind lift the curtains, I got very progressive and wondered almost aloud why I had the feeling something finally *was* happening. I couldn't have told Theenie nothing was happening then, because it was, something was. Then I knew that what I couldn't tease Theenie about was Taurus, and not because she wasn't there to tease, but because somehow he was much larger or worse or more significant than TV and the gubmen, and it wouldn't have been

teasing but something clearly unchildlike for me to
bring him up. And I thought it would kind of profane
him too, and somehow also the Doctor, who was
going without her maid and holy folded linen and
vacuumed floors to have him in the shack when she
didn't, I think, even see him two times for five
minutes in a week. And somehow it would profane
Daddy too—and the Doctor *and* Daddy, even though
by public decree they had done that one up brown
already—if I said two words to her about this alleged
grandbaby. Seeing Daddy's car parked a little
crooked in the driveway and knowing not to hear
what I heard was important too in this new kind
of event which presents or contains no action. And
even somehow Preston and Jinx and Jake and all the
Negroes who ran up to me when I rolled into the
oak tree like the low country's own gold-medal
gymnast, and looked at me in a way that was un-
eventful but magic, like I was not just a traffic
casualty but a special thing to them, connected to
this series. Somehow they would all be insulted if
I went about trying to sift action out of what I considered actionless events. If I pursued this racial
question on him any more than anyone else was, or
insisted on knowing more than I knew, it would
have been like charging into the marsh with a coffee
can to catch the fiddlers, and they would have de-
fended their secrets, waving their tiny ivory swords
and backing into their holes, and you'd be sucking
through the pluff mud like a fart machine. And you'd
come out green with mud and oyster cut, and with
an empty can.

Maybe that's why he gave me the assignment to

check out the Diane Parkers of this world, so I would be occupied, but I doubt he knew how fast I'd get to something like the mayonnaise. God, I feel like you could hear one too many mayonnaise revelations too early and go back to thinking people should be like dolls between their legs if it was going to be so damned complicated, which I thought once in my childhood mode.

But anyway, the Doctor has Taurus, or whomever if I hadn't named him, in Theenie's shack; Theenie's probably weaving baskets again, on the q.t. for TV crews; Daddy's trying these radically new-toned custody junkets on me; and I'm about lidding-out over several things that aren't even things—like mayonnaise, secretary's bazongas, motos, funny-parked cars.

But the center of the storm, calm as it was, was Taurus.

Chemistry Never Changes

✻ / So, it foundly occurred to me plenty was happening. That's a childhood thing I said, "foundly" for "finally." The best language is then. I knew a kid that called noses "noogs" and knives "niges" and a term like "big deal" he shorthanded "bih-deel *boing*!"—very fast with a blow of his fist on something like your head at the terminal sound.

Anyway, my little run of non-events suddenly was a veritable domino-phenomeno. What waked me up? Another crooked-parked car. There it was again, Friday, parked close up. I imagine six-inch angry skid marks just behind the tires. Daddy was early and inside *again*.

A little bud told me not to try the trick of listening at the door and then stomping in on an innocent note. He said stick my head up into the intake duct.

When we got the place from Eisenhower the Developer, it had a $5,500 Carrier cool-heat unit on a concrete pad under the house. The first season, the first hint of a hurricane, the first trickle of a high tide, that was it for Carrier. *Gihhhjjjj* POW—

magnesium flares, house trying to hop up and run away on its stilts, transformer blown off the pole by the hard road (you could hear it), and no power for three days anywhere out here. Candlelight at the Grand! That was most pleasant. Jake said he'd never seen rowdy niggers so serene.

So they yanked it—looked like a burned-out army tank. They gave the Doctor a replacement price and she gave them a drink of ice water and me a Girlhood speech: "Honey, when I was little, we didn't have all this. Just consider we're going back through Margaret Mitchell's wind."

To get some of that wind, we spent half a day bruising our hands trying to crack windows loose from their paint, and the sliding doors had these miniature locks down in the runners that Theenie said to prize out. "Prize 'em out with a crowbar or call the lock man, because you ain' gone get nare one out with this hammer." She had a hammer with one claw left, like a kid with a front tooth knocked out. She held it in an attitude that looked like one of those Walker Evans photographs of sharecroppers.

Theenie's got the sharecropper patience that seems so sure of the world even in its humility that the Doctor, who I thought would take out glass and all before calling anybody, stopped and called Vergil at the Texaco station and told him to get a locksmith who didn't have to have an arm and a leg and who might like a drink after a long day and bring him on out and to look at the Cadillac himself (Vergil), and she got them so well lubed there was no bill at all and we had those drapes standing out in the breeze in no time, like the capes of flying superheroes. And the roaring crowd of the surf was brought in—we had only heard the muffled rumble of it before.

Well, they pulled the burned hull of the heat pump and left all the ductwork, thinking the Doctor would change her mind about ordering a new unit. They didn't know she was one of these readers of Southern literature who talk about progressive light changes at dusk and how the air in the country is different than in the city, and how country crickets sing a different, more authentic tune than city crickets, who just get in your woodwork and keep you awake. It was many things like this that earned her the Duchess status.

So there was this square vent with silver insulation that came down to within four feet of the slab and I could stand on a block and go up in it to my shoulders. It was like putting your head in a speaker cabinet. You could hear the Doctor move on the wicker. It sounded like when a bad folksinger changes chords and the squeak on the frets is louder than the picking. You could hear the whole house, a giant conch shell and its internal sea. You could hear, believe me, voices.

So this Friday in question I get on the block and go shoulder-high into the Voice of the Theater.

". . . can*not* be h-wealthy forum," Daddy was saying.

". . . cannot buttabean h-wealthy forum," the Doctor said. I think I was too far up in the speaker.

". . . whoever evah hearded of a dearded child uvah twelvild runnnwellve vilding inilda nigger road nigoadhouse rrrouse!"

"I havehv."

"You're un*fit* tittit . . ."

I stepped down and moved the block and just stood under the vent, maybe only my hair up in it.

"Everson, frankly the place worried me too, before. But he *has* to have some life other than . . ." A small wicker squeak.

"Than what?"

"Than this." A big wicker squeak. This was much clearer.

"Well, *what* pray tell doesn't worry you *now*? Before *when*?"

"Before he had his new companion to—escort him."

"Companion. And not the first—"

"Don't start that tape—"

"I'll start it—"

"You're a boor."

A giant scraping and tinkling and gushing, pouring noise came down.

"Here. The ice is gone," Daddy said.

"Thanks."

It was quiet for so long I got scared they might be sneaking down. I could see the stairs where their shoes would show up long before they could see me, but I went over to the stairs just in case. Then they started talking again. I tiptoed back over, missed a few words.

". . . think either one of us," she said, and a pause like for a lecture notetaker, "has been *chaste*, has we, Iv?"

"In my book discretion still beats valor."

"Quite," she said. A scream of wicker. "So what

sets us so far apart in this spectrum of morals, my
lovely?" (Sounds weird, but that's what I heard.)

"That *I* don't with every coroner, convict, drifter,
and what's more entrust a boy to—"

"Who fucking *left*, Everson?" The volume nearly
scalped me. I was weak. I can only think of one noise
like that—a gun went off in a pawnshop on King
Street and it was like the air itself was black for a
moment, and we weren't even inside the shop. I
eased back up into the tube.

". . . if there's a difference. One leaves, one
doesn't. You couldn't, I could. Don't make me
out . . ."

"I know." An easy whine of wicker.

"Same?" Another chinking and wash sound.

"It's none of your business, but I'll tell you anyway. He came out here and found Theenie in her
gin and she decided he's her long-lost grandchild by
her crazy daughter." Still another punctuation of
glass and liquid noise. "And I asked him to stay here.
For Simons."

"You don't know him from—"

"Everson, did I know you? Did you know—"

"That was just for marriage. This, you've got, he's
raising—"

"Necessity of invention." Then, quickly: "Okay,
look. I liked the kid. At school the gossip mill has
done about as hysterical a thing as you want to.
God, this is strong. Look, Iv, we're all coming down
a bit, but I'm not addled yet. And the thing on
Simons, the book thing . . ."

"The book thing," he said.

"It's no good without the baseball thing." Then

she adds: "That's why the man's here, known or not. He's duty-free, cuts a figure, keeps him straight. That's all there is."

I'd had enough. All I had to do was figure out how to model my face for going in the house. This was some of the strangest verbiage I ever heard. I don't know why I thought so at the time. It looks reasonable now.

But I was hypered out, so I walked all the way back up to the Grand. When I was almost an hour late I called them.

"Where are you?"

"I'm up at Jake's. I thought Daddy could pick me up here."

"It's *your* weekend," she said. "When he gets here I'll tell him."

"Okay. Thanks." Thanks for mendacity, I should have said—mendacity and lies.

Well, I got a cold one. For the first time I needed one, I thought. I rolled it on my forehead. It felt like a new kind of ironing, heavy cold metal to smooth things out.

Jake came up and shook the can and put another one up without asking, like I was a real regular customer. "Drink dis slow. Your momma called, said sit tight."

I sat tight. After that one I didn't need to iron my head anymore.

I thought of a joke, for some reason, that Margaret Pinckney told during the last party. Bill and Jim interfered with her but she got it out, talking like a harelip. The hero's a harelip. Selling peaches, he knocks on a lady's door. She answers in "something comfortable—*very*," Margaret said.

"Yes?"

"Ma'am, want thum peacheth?"

"It would depend."

"Depend on what?" said the harelip.

"Are they firm?"

"Oh yeth, ma'am, they're firm."

"Do they have a very light fuzz on them?"

"Oh yeth, ma'am, they have a very light futh on them."

"Come in," the lady said, and he did.

"Are they as firm as these?" she asked, showing him her titties. Margaret said boobs.

"I couldn't thay."

She made him feel them. "Oh yeth, ma'am, they're ath firm ath theeth."

"Well, is the fuzz on them as light as this fuzz?" Margaret said: "She revealed herself totally to the harelip door-to-door peach salesman."

"I—I—I couldn't th-thay that either," he said.

"Give me your hand and we'll find out," she said, and then, jumping, said, "Quick, I hear someone coming! Under the sofa!"

The salesman rolled under the sofa and the lady dressed. It was a false alarm. When the heat blew off she got the salesman out.

"Whew."

"I'll thay." They settled down.

Then the lady said: "I'll buy *all* your fruit if you'll tell me what part of my body you think is the sharpest."

"The tharpetht?"

"Yes. And I'll take it *all*."

"Well, ma'am, I believe it'th your eerth."

"My *ears*?"

"Yeth, ma'am."

"But why my ears?"

"Well, you know when you thaid you thought you heard thomeone coming?"

"Yes."

"Well"—he hesitated—"it wath me."

It wath a houthe rocker that night. Even Bill and Jim were giggling. Why did I remember that, sitting in the Grand working on my second cold one? My first true second beer in my life.

Daddy came in.

"Mist'Iv," people said. "Mist'Iv!" I guess they knew him from their troubles. Daddy took their cases on time, I thought. Or they just knew he was the Duchess's old man. But anyway, he came in and had Jake's attention before he got to the bar and handed Jake a bottle in a sack.

"Do you have soda?"

"Got Coke soda," Jake said.

"Water then, Jacob."

Jacob. I had the feeling he'd been there before, or knew him somehow, which was a hard sensation to accept, like believing that sexy things are not your own private province of knowledge, that your parents must know too. Here I thought Jake and the Grand were all mine, and Daddy's calling Jake Jacob, like they go back years into a formal history together.

"Hi. Sorry if I'm in trouble," I said to cut him off, in case I was. "You know Jake?"

Jake handed up a jigger of whiskey and a jelly glass with tap water in it. Daddy nodded down. Jake nodded up.

"His father." Daddy was about titrated out. His lips were under control except they sort of looked like he'd been to the dentist. His eyes were mullety. "This place is just a juke joint now, son. In my day, it was the biggest whorehouse-casino-bootleg operation we knew of. Do you know what a whorehouse is?"

"Well, I know what one *is*. I don't know what you *do*, though."

He chased the jigger.

"Me either." He laughed.

We sat there a while.

I had a bunch of questions about the joint before, under Jake's daddy, but they seemed like too much effort. I could just put it together myself, with a hint or two.

"Daddy, was it what they call a class operation?"
"What?"

"Jake's joint in the good old days."

"Class operation is right!" He got excited. "That's *exactly* what it was. Everything was clear. They had the fun and we had the money. Buyers, sellers."

"*Refined* vice?" I said.

"What?"

"Like Chicago and things. Was it refined vice with a code of manners—"

"Son, do you believe in God?"

"What?"

"Do you believe in God?"

"Yeah, I guess."

"Well, okay. I guess it was refined vice."

I motioned to Jake and got my first true third cold one in my life. Daddy had said something I couldn't figure out. Today I sort of know. And I sort of don't.

Anyway, we left together and drove home to the Cabana. And he stayed there that night. I didn't need any air ducts to know that.

"God, Iv," I heard come from their room.

"God what?"

"Chemistry."

"Chemistry what?"

"Chemistry never changes."

And then a set of rock groans no oracle ever bettered. And I'm drunk, which probably made it worse. And if chemistry never changes, why'd they split up? I guess somebody could wonder that, but it's probably only me, drunk. Everyone who knows them says they split up because the Doctor's a bitch, if they are on his side, and because the Progenitor's an asshole, if they're on hers, and some people say both. That leaves me to wonder. I don't. I know.

The Doctor is a Democrat and the Progenitor is a Republican. I don't mean registered voters now, I mean their whole attitude. They both voted for Nixon, so it's not that simple. They both vote for Nixon but she thinks it's a land where you decide your boy is a novelist and feed him books and he *is* one, and he thinks in these supply-demand curves and says book reading's fine but there will have to be baseball for balance and law school in order that I be a producer and not a ward of the state, and *bam*—they are in it, fighting in a corner.

"He's bright enough. Let him read if he wants to."

"He has to *work* on it, Iv."

"He's a boy, for God's sake."

"Not any boy. *My* boy."

Crack!

"If you hit me again, it'll be the last time."

I wondered about that one for years. How did he do it? A short, deft blow that broke her nose? A high-handed Cagney slap? Or a schooled punch, like a hook? We boxed, twice. He got me these gloves the size of plums and put them on me and placed my guard and said keep your guard up and come on. I did, with whirring weightless arms, concentrating on his T-shirt near his armpits, enveloping him in a storm of bad ideas until he reached out and thumped my mouth and I quit.

So what he did to her I don't know. I did not see any mark the next day. But I knew that in a universe alleged to contain only men who beat their wives and men who don't, he was a doer. At least he was in principle, because I'm not sure one shot is a true beating. It wouldn't be if she had cracked him one, which for all I know she was trying to do, like me, swinging away, when he produced the audible whap.

They could have this same kind of talk about business or money or careers or jobs, which is why I say their differences fall under the loose heading of political.

"I sold the Market Street property," he'd say.

"You *what?*"

"I sold it."

"*Without consulting me?*"

Silence. Then she orates: "If it weren't for me,

you wouldn't—*we* wouldn't—have two quarters to rub together. I'm through with you." A sweeping noise of drink and napkin, a cabinet door slams, she heads for the bedroom, door locks. He must sit there with a solid look on his face. He mixes another drink.

Once, though, they worked up to the ignition point, and she said, "It's over. Get out."

"Hell, it's my house. You get out." And beat her to the bedroom. That one tickled me.

But it's still kind of hard to lie there hearing all this, even though some of it's funny. Too much of it's about you, in the third person, when they could just get you in there for your opinion instead of relegating you to misfit. Hell, I would have told them all they needed to know. They'd have both been jaked up if they had asked me. I don't know how they ever managed to dream that they had an object, like a commodity on a market they had to invest this way or that. And finally, there was a feeling I had that they had quit being themselves in favor of *my* becoming themselves, as if they were sacrificed to me. They assumed this sacrifice willingly together and only later discovered there were two lives being gambled on one.

So imagine the impact of my falling out of a bus, suspected of smoking modern hemp with Negro kids, and my taking up with a process server nobody knows a thing about but Theenie, who swears he's the evil incarnation of her lost heroin grandbaby out of her bad-jazz-singer crazyass daughter. Imagine that. And I think all that carrying on on my part necessitated some immediate investment consultations, changed the curve of custody junkets, invigorated faculty parties, sweetened my last hours at Jake's Baby Grand, for I knew a chapter was closing, and imperiled, of course, my friendship with the process server I got to even name like he was a character in those novels I was supposed to write.

A Saturday without Cartoons

🪰 / The next morning Daddy was still there and I was sort of glad, but more certainly embarrassed, and in a way entirely different from coroner embarrassment. I'd got used to that. I could dismiss them with a marshaling of my lips into what I considered a pucker of disgust. But now the Progenitor was with Penelope. Great Olympic siren squeals had issued forth from the rocks of their bed. A coroner I hated was one thing, but now it was a guy I had a relationship with, like a very good friend in there—a guy who told me a rubber is like a sock. It hypered me out. About 6 a.m. I tried the hamburger and fishing broadcast and then hit the beach to get out of there.

Taurus wasn't at the shack, but I saw some smoke up at the abandoned Boy Scout camp and kept walking. It was Taurus, with a fire lit up under a triangle-shaped coffeepot, like in a cowboy movie. It was just like the open range. He was stoking dead palmetto fronds in. You could smell the coffee. It almost had a scorchy smell.

I was going to go up like a drifter and ask for some grub and do a movie parody, but didn't. He just handed me a cup. I was drinking it before I realized I hate coffee and then realized I didn't hate it anymore, and that those first three true cold ones had probably produced my first true hangover and had changed coffee, like liquor, into something to drink, not to fake-drink with milk. Did he know about this, my blowout?

The fire was down quickly, because the fronds burn so fast, and I got up to pull a Sabal branch. I had to about swing on it to get it loose, and when I did I fell with it, and on the ground beside me was a sparrow, dead. He was still able to move his head if you did it for him. I couldn't figure out where he came from—under the branch, in the shelter they make against the tree? Was he in there and I some-how killed him? Or was he already on the ground and I didn't see him?

"You seen this bird before?"

"No," he said.

"I think I killed him."

"I wasn't really looking, though."

"He . . . you can still move him. I must have."

He didn't say anything more, so we drank coffee.

"The oracle at the heating system spoke of great new formations in my fate," I said. "There are what you might have to call propitious portents."

"What would they be?"

"It looks like Daddy's back."

"That's good."

"It's good?"

"Sure it's good."

"You know him?"

"Heard his name around. Serving."

"Never met him?"

"No."

"I seem to know this means you'll be going."

"Could."

"How is that?"

"What?"

"That you'll have to go."

He looked at me. I was blabbering. It was one of those times where you're supposed to act indifferent, or knowing, to what you don't know. I saw these ninth-graders pull it off by keeping their traps shut one night on a school-bus field trip and kissing the cheerleaders instead of yapping like younger kids with no one to kiss. All you had to do was shut up and the girls got very adult about you.

"Well, like Frank Zappa said."

"What'd he say?" It worked. I turned him into the curious one.

"That's where it's *at*, baby."

He said nothing—turned the table again.

"Yessiree-bob," I appended. "Yessireebob."

There was the funny pot and the sparrow.

"Look," I said, "I don't want to get lugubrious but I have to say it—I'll miss you, we've had my most fun in my life, so thanks."

"Me too, Sim."

"Annh . . . let's gedattaheah," I said.

"Let's bury this vulture you slew."

We did.

Mullet

🦟 / "Before you go off to the middle of nowhere we better go fishing, to ratify our experience together," I said.

So I stopped off at the Cabana and got two mullet specials all fixed up. You need a long pole in case they're deep. Not too small a hook. The idea that mullet have small mouths is specious. It's actually part of a racist wives'-tale scheme of lies which relegates mullet as fish to a similar position known by Negroes as people, but we don't have time for all that. Their mouths are plenty large is all. But delicate, so you have to pull them in a firm but not exuberant fashion. (Also part of this bogus press on mullet is they don't even bite hooks, which is already a bit obvious in its error, or I wouldn't be under the house untangling cane poles and rusty hooks.) And a cork—not too big there. You want a good, subtle cork, preferably a thin one capable of doing things other than simply going under, because most mullet

will not take a cork under. The cork should be able
to shiver.

We took off to get worms. The best place is behind the Grand, by Jake's old house, where you're
supposed to believe there was a still, and I suppose
there was. There's plenty of worms, I know that. You
have to go in through the Grand, where Jake will be
cleaning up, and tell him, and he'll never say a word
of greeting. You just tell him and he calls his mother,
who still lives there, and she'll chain up that pit
bulldog which I said had mice in his ears the day I
began becoming famous. Mice in his ears or not, it
is a very crazy dog that tightens out this chain from
a log truck.

"The story is they dumped the mash in this pit,"
I told Taurus. "All the corn and potatoes and vegetables they couldn't eat went in the mash. Here they
use anything. Or did. I don't think anybody runs one
now. They just get the bootleg stuff without tax
stamps. It's the modern world."

"Where's a shovel?" he said.

"You can't shovel worms," I said. "It's too gross."

So I showed him how you have to use your fingers
if you care about the worms or you'll have half a
mash pit of halved worms.

"Another thing, you can't profane this mash pit,
because of Jake's boy."

"Who's Jake's boy?"

"He's Jake's boy, but it's on the q.t. because he's in
Bull Street in the retard section. I've never seen him.
The story is, they fed him the wood chips for color-
ing the shine and he ate them like potato chips and

that did it. All they meant to do was kind of slow him down so they didn't have to mind him so close, but it slowed him down further than they figured."

Taurus was combing worms out of the leaves like a pro. Big ones fighting all over the leaves between his knees, and he was picking them up without even taking any detritus, so I put a dirt wad in the can for their shade.

"I think it was red oak," I said. This is a guess, because I never could learn what kind of wood they really used. "Red oak because not too much sap but a nice reddish color, like real whiskey, and then they'd pull the chips out and suck on them like a martini olive, only Jake's boy was undersized, so he sort of O.D.'d. Nobody talks about him much."

We got over to Horry Slough, where I thought the mullet would be, and they weren't. It's a good place usually. When the tide's out all you see is pluff mud slick and olive-green and drilled full of fiddler holes. It has a nice salt stink, and the mud actually *ticks*—you can hear it—in the sun. When the tide's full you'd never know the place: blue water brimming up to green saw grass like a postcard, and a million mullet jumping like tiny tarpon. But all Taurus and I saw was two Negro ladies sitting hopelessly in the sun on their buckets. I watched them not get any bites.

"When they sposed to start biting?" I said.

"They might not be sposed to," one of them said, laughing.

"Did they bite yesterday?"

"*Might* did."

I was trying to find out if they were operating on information or on faith. It looked like faith.

"Have ya'll seen anybody fishing anywhere else?" I said.

"A bunch of 'um at the pier," she said.

"Wheat and Lilly ovadeah," the other one said.

"Wheat? He out the hospital?" the first said.

"Shomuss *be*."

The thing you can't do with Negro ladies fishing is expect them to care very much about immediate success, theirs or yours. There could be a hundred people hauling them in tuna style at that pier and they wouldn't pick up and ride over there like most people would. It violates something. I've never figured it out. They will sit there and sweat and their worms will cook in the can and get too pink-soft and stinky to stay on the hook and they won't catch a fish and later will hear about all the fish Wheat and Lilly caught and will not despair. It's magic, that kind of control, maybe like Theenie's live-till-you-die program. Or they *will* catch some fish, three bream that wouldn't crowd a coffee cup, and keep them and fry them hard as toast and still not despair, eating them in five bites of exploding greasy cornmeal and bones and salt.

But we couldn't stay there without despair setting in, so I adjourned us to the action at the county pier, out where the river is wider. Pulling up, we saw a heavy woman at the corner of the pier set her hook and haul a mullet over the silver guardrail. And a man was riding down the pier on a three-wheeled bicycle. He passed us. In his baskets he had sacks and boxes and empty pop bottles and an open bucket full of mullet in pink slime.

"Mornin'," he said, and kept pedaling.

"Wheat!" the heavy woman shouted, without turning but yelling at the river. "Hurry up!"

He jammed the front wheel sideways like a trailer jackknifing and had to get off to straighten it out. He doddered around the bike like Charlie Chaplin in slow motion. He could hardly walk.

Meanwhile, the woman had corralled the mullet flipping all over the pier and sat on it. "Hurry wid dat bucket!" She was laughing and all the others— about three—were, too, but quietly, all still watching their corks.

There was another guy on the pier, a white guy. He was off at a remove from the ladies, who were sitting with their arms through the guardrail—they have to haul the fish over their heads without getting up. The guy was standing, his line far out on the bottom. He was not fishing for mullet. Of course. They chap my ass. It's one thing to niggerize a fish and think little of it but here's an asshole who goes out into a mullet run and turns up his nose at them in public. He was red-colored and knotty-looking. Mr. James has his famous line about a kind of guy *would* have been a redhead? Well, this kind of guy would have been a stepchild named Psoriasis. Except somebody named him Billy. Or Billy Ray. Or Billy Ray Bob. Billy Ray Bob Wally Pickett.

Next he starts mumbling real chummy about "Lilly, I bleve you gone catch all the fish in the river!"

"Shih, I hope so," she says back, obligated.

What he's really saying is, "I hope you catch all the stinking mullet while I catch a good fish," it's clear. Or he'd reel in and bait up short and start catching mullet himself. There is something to do to this kind of guy but I don't yet know what it is. But this Lilly seems to know.

Right in the middle of this happy talk with Psoriasis, she picks up an Old Milwaukee beer by her hip and tilts it up on her face and gags.

"This beer kissy hot!" She looks for Wheat, who's still doddering. "Kissy hot! Buckwheat!"

Wheat's almost remounted and he makes the several pedals necessary to pull up behind Lilly.

"You so slow, no wonder your wife left you," she shouts at the river.

"She din' leave me," Wheat says. "She died."

"The ultimate *leff*," Lilly says, and they howled, all the ladies. Even Wheat giggled.

"Well, where *is* it?" Lilly says.

"Wheah whah?"

"The cold beer!"

"Hold your horse." Wheat digs into the bicycle basket. Past fried chicken in a shoebox with wax paper, and some stray mullet all mixed in with the chicken, old paper sacks, and cardboard, through fishing tackle too, corks and tangled lines and hooks, empty beer cans, finally he pulls out a six-pack of Old Milwaukee. Paper is stuck to it because it's sweating.

"Goddamn, Buckwheat!" Lilly yells.

"Goddamn whah!" Wheat yells back.

"It's gone be kissy hot, too. Where's the ice?"

"The ice?"

"You forgot the ice!"

"No, I din'. I must over*looked* it."

Another howl.

"Well, gimme the bucket."

Wheat starts to lift out the bucket of mullet and she sees him struggling with it. "Well, that fits. You spose to put them at the house."

"I cuhn," he says.

"Why you *cuhn*?"

"Iss lock. You din' give me no *key*." There is a victorious thrust in his voice.

"Well, give me a beer, you old fool."

Wheat tears loose a beer.

Lilly hands him the key and the mullet she's sat on.

He puts the mullet in the bucket and mounts up and starts to go and then stops. "Say, Needa," he says. Another lady answers. "You gone to the church Friday?"

"Friday. For what?"

"For the wedd'n."

"Wedd'n? Who gettin' marrit?"

"Me." There's a titter from the ladies.

"You? Who gone marry you?"

"I thought *choo* was." A big howl. Buckwheat pedals off.

So we finally got to see some mullet action. It turned out Lilly was a pro. She had the timing down. Mullet fishing is timing—more timing I'd say than sheephead fishing, though it's close. When the mullet

comes up to the ball of worms—a big gob, I prefer—
he must do something to the worms like a duck does
to silt and algae. First a gentle mouthing and then a
fierce gumming and sucking. Which makes the cork
just shiver. If it moves it's because it accidentally
gets hung up and moves off with the mullet. Usually
it just shivers. That's when you have to hit him, and
firmly, but not horse-rough. It's an art to nail a fish
and then relax without letting the authority escape.
Especially a mullet, which is a thinking fish—you
have to let him know you know how delicate his
mouth is but that he's creelbound all the same and
no funny stuff. I'm good at it, but that Lilly was a
pro.

I was watching old Psoriasis down there when she
set the hook and doubled her pole, and whatever she
had hooked remained solidly deep and moved sideways at a good clip. Lilly strained up, making her
pole whine. It still stayed down. Usually you have a
mullet out in one smooth motion.

Lilly yelled to the river, "Gahad damn!" and everybody watched the deepness move to her right. She
pulled even harder, the pole tip itself in the water, a
bamboo semicircle connecting Lilly on the pier to
the river, quivering and ticking like a dowser. Then
it came up. It was only a mullet foul-hooked in the
belly. She thought she had the biggest mullet of all
time. Psoriasis was down there sucking his teeth,
his sorry excuse for a laugh. The other ladies all
said what they had thought. Lilly said what she had
thought.

I baited Taurus up and my own and caught one

during their analysis—not too big but big enough
to offer the ladies, which would buy our way into
the fishing hole without any resentment. I also
thought we could pique old Psoriasis, but then I
realized it would be better to be seen keeping some
mullet for ourselves—that would fry his butt
better.

"We might keep a couple," I said to Lilly, "just to
eat tonight. But we won't need the rest and ya'll can
have them." Fine, fine. It's a good way to get bait
insurance, this, too. You're giving somebody fish and
run out of bait, and unless he's a fool he will supply
you with some.

Taurus did very well for his first trip—caught
three mullet and a red bass, which got everybody,
even Psoriasis, excited. The first time I went for
mullet I was skunked, because I waited for the cork
to go under. "He won't under it, child," a woman
finally said.

"He won't take it *un*der?"

"No. Watch it close. It'll shiver like. Then pull
hard."

"How hard?"

"Not too hard."

I was confused, because they were laying back
like tuna men for no apparent reason cork-wise. (I
heard this local news guy say, "That's the way it
crumbles, cookie-wise.")

Anyway, I caught five or six, including two big
ones, which I announced we would keep, and held
up at Psoriasis, who looked away at his line, which
hadn't had a bump. "Ya'll keep the rest, and this

red bass," I said, and dropped it loudly into their
bucketful of sad-eyed slimy mullet.

And so Taurus and I went home for the last
supper, a meal of two old mullet with hemorrhages
in their jaundiced eyes, pouting up at us like their
dogs had died.

A *Vision* of *Snug Harbor*

✦ / Then we went to town one last time, for no reason other than the good old days, which you could taste suddenly getting closer to their end and sweeter, like the last pieces of candy. We got up early on a Saturday I was not scheduled for a custody junket. Taurus had his car idling by the shack, mumbling little piffs of hot smoke into the cool cloud of fog which held everything still like a sharecropper photograph. We closed the green shutters on the sea window and one of them fell off, about breaking my foot. I said before they were sorry shutters anyway, which he got from Charleston, and they were sorry even though no dime-store stuff. Each weighed about a hundred pounds, which is why the one fell and why they never departed this world in the hurricanes which probably took a house or two out from under them. That's why Taurus could come to find them out of service yet still for sale, shutters stouter than planters' summer homes and stronger than a cotton economy. When that one fell in the sand, old and spent as it had to

be, with scaling paint so thick it could cut your
fingers like can lids, it looked like the top of a
treasure chest to me. It was green and crooked, with
sand already drifting into the louvers.

"Theenie's going to pitch a fit about cutting her
wall open," I said.

"We'll put it back later."

"It won't matter," I said. "When she gets back and
sees that hole, she'll put a mattress in it until we
get a professional carpenter with tar paper and tin
tabs and real lumber to shore it back up *right*."

"Hmmp," he said, just like Theenie. He was a
cool jake to the end. We took off.

We had breakfast at an old hotel on the Citadel
Square in Charleston. John Calhoun's out there in
bronze about forty feet tall, and it seems he's doing
something about the Confederacy by standing up
there so very proudly, but I don't know what, because I don't know what he did, if he was a decent
Reb or a bad one or anything. Looking out the cool
dewy windows of the hotel, feeling the cold glass, I
could still see that sad shutter in the sand.

We order these country-gentleman breakfasts, and
this other waitress than ours comes to the table. She
just comes up very close to it, even presses it with
her front, and just kind of turns her lips or bites the
inside corner of her mouth, tucking her lips to one
side.

"Hey," she says to Taurus, but then she looks
quickly at me, too. It's a funny way to show them,
but I get the idea this girl has manners.

Taurus stands up and takes her hand and bows
to kiss it, and she snatches it away with a laugh

and sort of slow-motion socks him in the arm. Then
she wiggles around like a tail wagging a dog. Her
uniform rear had some jelly on it, which she might
have already had or got wiggling, I don't know, but
it was funny the way she moved sideways to him
but watched him straight with large eyes. In fact,
they were the largest eyes I had ever seen that weren't
in a calf, and very blue or gray. I think I had a
romantic stirring.

"Are we all set?" Taurus asked.

"I don't know," she said.

He doesn't say anything. She fiddles with the table
a bit. "She's never been on a date, T."

Who? T.? I was figuring a bunch of things at the
time, like the eminent sensation I had that this
female third party had a lot to do with me, so I
missed for a time the significance of "T." That's
what she called him for short, I guessed, and it became my only clue to his real name, because that's
all she called him and I never asked. But could he
really *have* been named Taurus?

"Well," he says. "Simons here is just starting out
himself."

"Oh, good." Then she adds, "That's romantic,"
almost so quiet you can't hear her.

"You get off at eleven? We'll be down there on the
green."

We got those country-gentleman breakfasts with
pork chops that had about an ounce of paprika and
pepper on them, very tasty, and cut them up in
white-sided chunks and pushed the rich broken egg
yolks around, making the meat yellow. I was all of
a sudden hungry as hell.

"What's happening?"

"We're going sailing," he told me. "With a boatful of willing gentlewomen from the low country."

"Holy God."

"Holy God is right."

Suddenly great old patinaed John Calhoun and the green shutters all vanished before what I was sure was the dawning of the real, present South, a new land full not of ghosts but of willing gentlewomen.

It didn't turn out so marvelous. It's like water-skiing, which is no fun until you know what you're doing. Same with kissing, etc. We picked up this girl from a house on the Battery. She was cute all right, a regular button of a girl. She jumped down the steps in blue tennis shorts and a white cotton shirt with a tiny monogram, her hair pulled back, making her face shinier than it might have been without the tension, which was, I suspected, plenty shiny. She had on blue Keds that looked tight too and little pom-pom socks. She jumped in the car. For some reason, before I could look at her face all I saw was those cinched-up shoes, brand-new and looking as firm as shoe forms or hooves. I wondered if I was going to be a blockhead.

The trouble was, Taurus's girl was shabby where mine was shiny, loose where mine was tight, and I had already taken a heavy fall for her because of those jaw-breaker eyes. And she was developed out. Now, I didn't hold that against mine, because my burning worm was nothing to call the bureau of standards and measures about either, but the whole effect of this big-eyed, wobbling, nervous girl with giant bazongas had got to me, and what I wanted was a little one just like her. What I had looked like something at a recital.

"Oh, wait!" she cried, clapping her hand to her mouth. "Hi" to me. "I forgot" to them. She dropped a pink orthodontic retainer from the roof of her mouth and was out of the car and up the steps and back, smiling, in one motion. "All set."

She and I got through names and grades before we reached the water. We were about even on names —she was a double Jenkins and I had my one-"m" Simons, plus the Manigault—but on schools she had the edge, being at Mrs. Oldfield's famous institution for landed white girls, while I was in Bluffton Elementary with the people. I was going to display some Great Books stuntwork if she pressed about my not going to Cooper Boyd Academy. But she didn't. She was nervous and smiling so hard about nothing at all that every time I looked at her, it sort of hurt my face. I hoped a little weather and salt on the boat would knock the shine off and we could be regular. Her name was Londie. Short for Altalondine Jenkins Jenkins.

At the yacht club we met a gigantic fat dude who was breathing with difficulty. He outfitted us with his boat, an air of a favor he owed Taurus about the proceedings. He made sure to impress Taurus with how irregular lending his boat was without *his* going. And then Taurus's girl came out of the yacht club changed into a purple swimsuit with plenty of everything very obvious and she a little self-conscious, which made her smile and do that dog-wobble ever so slightly. On the front of the suit was a brilliant whale dancing on its fluke and spouting white spume, the figure made of inlays of nylon stitched together in colors resembling a parrot. The fat guy stopped talking when he saw her.

I watched him while Taurus rigged the boat. He had been blubbering about tightening this and battening that and rules of the road, but now he was mostly pointing and grunting, half at Taurus and half at his girl. His wheezing picked up.

He stepped over to Taurus and said, "My health."

Taurus looked up.

"I'm worried about my health."

"What about it?" Taurus said.

He sucked in a big load of wind and said, "It's *deteriorating*."

Taurus was holding a broken halyard and standing in three inches of stinking bilge water in the open ribs of the cockpit.

"What *isn't*?" he said.

"Good point! Very good point! Ah, sir!" shouted the wheezer. He laughed and then charged Taurus's girl, virtually shouting, "Young lady! There's a *whale* on your stomach!"

She bit her mouth sideways, stretched her suit outward a bit, and looked down at the colorful whale.

"Are you a"—he almost choked—"a *swimmer*?" With reverence in that word.

She looked at him and then at herself again, up and down, her legs, the whale, the bosom she could hardly see over. Now I was excited too, but the big guy was, I swear, fixing to collapse drooling, and she was getting red in the face. He was about two

inches from her and standing like Santa Claus,
rocked back on his heels with an enormous gut stuck
out, which he rubbed absently with tiny hands, and
he looked at her through eyes squinted shut with fat,
seething, when Taurus said to her, "In the boat."
And to me, "Cast off." She did, I did, Londie jumped
in as light and precise as a fawn, and we motored
out of the club.

That was about the biggest adventure of the day.
It got a little rough, but nobody puked. We kept our
stomachs full with cold Coca-Cola and nice big
chunks of ice. Coke can taste very good in salty
conditions, I've noticed.

We went to Fig Island, which is one island too
small for the Arabs to bother to take. It was nice.
We played in the water. Londie and I worked on our
kissing nerve by trying to swim at each other under-
water and embrace and then kiss, but each time
one or both of us burst out laughing in embarrassment before we got our lips situated, big blasts of
bubbles obliterating the target and the moment, and
we'd have to surface for air and laugh and laugh
more to conceal how scared we were to actually do it.
And then I saw something that really took the wind
out of my sails.

There was Taurus and his girl about a hundred
yards away in chest-deep water, and she had her
arms at full length draped on his shoulders, and
maybe it was a trick of light and water or something
but I swear I saw large pale surfaces between them
and I thought it was her tits floating. It destroyed
our game, made it so silly. I don't even know if it

was her tits, if boobs even float like that, if it wasn't a fish belly. But the idea was enough. Me and old A'londine was way down in the minors, so I suggested we walk the island.

It had a shell ring. That's a ring of oystershells piled about head-high in a circle about fifty yards across. Indians made them, they say for ceremonies and whatnot, and of course even live sacrifices get bandied about, but my information is that they don't really know. The rock hounds and anthropods come out and remove chunks of the rings like bites out of a doughnut, but I don't think they ever find anything but oystershells. The digs are all old-looking. My guess is it's where the Indians had their oyster roasts, and a fine way to use the shells too, because it cuts out the wind for 360 degrees.

Anyway, we thought about the ghosts of Indians and rumrunners and all those old things that took place on a coast, and we didn't really square off for the kissing like we wanted to. Just became regular jake friends while Taurus, etc. I felt little.

But at least he went to bat for me, and if I whiffed, it wasn't his fault, maybe not my fault, certainly not button-nosed Altalondine Jenkins's fault, and most certainly not that big wobbly blessing's fault, for if ever there was a walking incitement to riot she was it. Call her my first love, fine with me.

I think that was his plan, really, to show me not cutie-cakes but what you can find if you look for genteel Diane Parkers—big, wonderful, warm girls who are just a hint upset about things. A smudge of abandon. Maybe that's my motto. Me and old Mike can team up. He can worry about being an ignoramus and I can worry about round, wonderful girls with their edges ruined by life's little disasters, who remain solid and tough in their drive to feel good— to themselves and to you—and offer a vision of snug harbor.

Photos for the Record

☙ / We got back from sailing, still ratified by mullet. I said let's stop at this photo parlor. It was an ancient type, with medieval backdrops and little dull pictures of you about three for a dollar. We walked in and didn't see anybody.

"What *fer* ya?" comes from the rear of the hall. All we could see was amusement things, like punching bags with strength meters, pinball games, and the like, down both walls to darkness.

"Some photographs," I said. We had walked up on the speaker, who was sitting in a metal scallop lawn chair. Around him were a stove, refrigerator, TV, end tables, some fruit. We were in his living room.

"Sit down," he says. "It's hot."

"Yessir," Taurus says, "plenty hot."

There was his wife, too, in another scallop chair. She said, "Hmmp."

"You young Americans just sit down and give a account of y'self," the old guy says.

"This is sure one nice game hall," Taurus says.

"Hmmp."

"This, son?" The old man points around. "This a gyp joint, son."

We sat there.

"*Was* nice, once. Had a bunch more *in* it. Our daughter sells it off next door."

The wife chuckled. He looked at her. "What?"

"The bear," she said.

"Had this bear in here, she sold it, it would . . . you would squeeze it to show how strong you were on a dial thing. Only thing was, it squoze *back*."

She chuckled again.

"So we had a bunch a' navy come in here one day and a big boy got that bear and wouldn't give up and it broke bofe his ribs."

"Both?" I said.

"*Bofe* of 'em," he said happily, then he sobered up. "Time was, a thing like that was funny. They all left laughing like hell."

"Today you'd get sued," the wife said.

"Evathing changes." He looked around. "Boys, remember that. This ain't nothin' but a gyp joint. We just holding on. Evathang changes."

Then he drew near and looked Taurus in the eye. "We're from *Georgia*."

We sat there.

"Well, about those pictures," I said.

"Sho. Come on, come right on up. Me and Opal wasn't doing nothing but feeling sorry for ourself anyway."

We took snapshots in these Confederate scenes. I

thought we'd come out looking like J.E.B. Stuart and Nathan Bedford Forrest. Taurus looked like a criminal and I looked like a mole. But we had them photographs.

In this old real snapshot we have (you can tell it's old by the beer can I use—it has rims visible on the end, and it's bitten open by the turtle-beak shapes of a church key), I am pouring seawater on the Doctor, who is lying face down in the sand. The water is frozen glisteny, one inch from hitting her. And I have this smile and kind of nervous-looking feet and legs, like I know I'm going to have to run. Well, the old man is off about six feet, I guess, watching this—he took the picture. I don't remember running. I don't remember ever wearing the dumb bathing suit they have me in, either. It's all crinkly and flimsy and baggy, like lettuce or something. But other than that, you can tell everything's fine. Daddy didn't shoot out of focus, or shake the camera, and didn't cut half the Doctor or me out with a bad aim. And she looks very serene, very settled, maybe beautiful. You can tell even I know it because, though my legs are nervous and ready, I'm very pleased with what I'm doing. I'm happy about it.

But later it's not so clear, things. I have another beach memory. I'm out in the water and all of a sudden the Doctor is waving me in and calling me. So I head in and she starts waving even harder—I see then she's not calling me *in*, but screaming me *out*. I wasn't even coming in when she started. It's most weird. There's a stir up the beach, I see, by an old boat. Daddy is over there and their guests. Well,

I can only get near enough to see Daddy shoot a pistol at the boat. Everything relaxes. I get past her then and up to the boat and he's shot a snake.

"Are you satisfied?" Daddy says to the Doctor.

"It's still alive," she says. Then to me: "Get back, Simons Everson!"

I take a step or two back.

"There was no need to kill it," Daddy says, and walks off.

Then I saw what I thought was guts on the sand start moving. The snake was twisting like a spring and I thought the guts were attached and that explained it. But the guts got two feet away, over unstained sand, and kept going. It was babies!

"You might have killed *it*," I called to them, "but you missed these here," and I was going to pick them up, they were very cute, when it really broke loose, the Doctor snatching at me hysterically and the old man kept walking, laughing, down to the beach. There's no photograph of that, of any of that.

A Revelation of Foolery

✿ / **W**ell. You knew he was a rake before you saw him courting women bosom-loosed in the swelling green sea, because, if for no better reason, he had learned that trick of keeping his mouth shut for the most part around women, like the varsity ninth-graders around cheerleaders. Except in their case it's a practiced move and in his it's genuine.

One day about a month before the Saturday we took Dietrich and the Princess sailing, I went up to the shack very early and before I knocked someone stepped from behind a palm holding a whiskey bottle, quiet and sure as a Pinkerton man on stake-out. It was Taurus.

It scared me so bad, this electric thing went off in my sac, which they call pissing in your pants, but it's different.

"Hey, fucker," I gasped, white.

"You're mighty early."

"Early bird gets the worm" was all I could say, since my heart had caught the electric jolt too. You

always have these hook-man convict stories on your
brain out here, and what with the constant wind,
you can't hear people move, so it's worse, and I'm
holding my heart.

Well, I didn't think much of it. But then when I
went up to go sailing, his car was idling and warm,
he was all set, practically closing those shutters before I got there, like he had seen me coming, and I
learned something about the early-bird morning. I
knew he had not *waited* to scare me. He had chased
me. He chased me and designed a calm steady
stepping into view from behind a tree to disguise
the pursuit. He followed me. From the Cabana. Then
it all started to fall in place.

It's funny how one minute you don't know a thing
and then something happens which in itself is not
telling but which serves nonetheless as a thump on
a long line of dominoes. And his closing that shutter
on the sailing day was the thump and they began
to fall. It was as early as the time before, if not
earlier, yet he was well ahead of me, not closing
from behind with whiskey in hand like a smoking
pistol. The whiskey was in a sack.

One night some time before, the Doctor had run
out of liquor and I told her Jake didn't carry her
stuff anymore, and besides, they had a saxophone
player in from a faraway place and of old local fame
and it would be packed. She hesitated a bit and then
went up on her toes over the refrigerator and opened
a small cabinet and drew out a bottle in a sack. I
even remember thinking how young her calves
looked flexed up, and not particularly about the
liquor being up there, which was the novel thing.

Nor did anything really dawn when I saw Taurus that morning with a sack just like it. But when we got back from sailing I went home, got on a chair, got to it, skinned the sack back, and Old Setter—his liquor—trembled in my hand. Penelope!

I cloistered the evidence and jumped down, knees buckling with confusion. No, actually I was sprightly. I had some of that electric hook-man thing in my nuts, but it was different from the fear electricity. This tickled a little.

I didn't know what to think. I holed up in my room, bassinet bound by books provided by my sweet mother. The entire Modern Library among other things, original glossy jackets on them. Trilogies, juvenilia, oeuvres! The works. I opened the window and unhooked the screen and dropped it off into the sand. Leaned back in a straight chair with my feet in the window, looked at the coquina beach, surf chomping, and took a steady gale of sand in the teeth while I sorted it out.

I had been consummately stupid! The whiskey was a lighthouse light over an entire reef of secrets. At night when I had thought myself asleep—now suddenly I could recall gentle sounds, innocent door knocks and paddings thereto and slipping bolts and whining hinges and paddings, softer and heavier, coming back. Whiskeys and ices tinkling and low, steady voices, twelve bells and all's well, and I must have been rolling over and off into turns of deeper, dreamless watch. Because now I knew there had been the bower sounds then too, the deep moaning of oracle rocks in the Carrier vents, sounds like blankets settling on cold patients, fluffed up in the air with a snap of woolen breath by healthy nurses and floating down on ailing folk to make them better, much better by morning. And how comfortable I felt, thinking it just the fun *I* was having with him, when it was more. It was fun *she* was having, and that mattered, I had to admit, and it mattered also when the Progenitor had come home and I consciously heard the Carrier moan, because then I did not want to call them the Progenitor and the Doctor but my mother and father, the way Jake would call his mother Momma when he went back to see her every afternoon before opening up, after he had cleaned up the joint, and they just sat on her porch.

So who was I going to blame? At first I thought him, for not telling me, but then he couldn't very well have advertised it or I'd have had him on the coroner list before long probably, and then I realized he did tell me, the same way he told me everything else, with one ounce of suggestion and pounds of patience. He didn't have to step out from behind a tree, he could have gone anywhere. He could have left that bottle at the Cabana, or thrown it away. And God knows he's a sport—I'd seen him release to warm Atlantic bay water the boundless bosom of my very own first girlfriend, though I hadn't managed more than three words to her and with any more would have come off like the fat dude, though on the flip side, seething with green innocence. He's a sport, he's game, and even I admit she's a good-looking broad even for your mother. And lonely, and all that. So I can't blame her—Taurus is a sight (and a damn sight) better than ten coroners boiled into one human being if you could do that.

So what was my complaint? My teeth were full of sand, mainly. I went down and got the screen and put it back in and tried to shake it off. Made a hamburger and a Coke, I was still full of salt from the sailing. The only thing was, I thought the Progenitor —Daddy—had been negotiating a return since that night he got me at the Grand. Was that true? When had I heard the "we'll be friends" conversation between Taurus and my mother? Was it over and done with before I caught on? Is that why he had to take my girlfriend from me? He was giving me my mother? And my father? Could he do that? I didn't know. I half wished he had given me my girlfriend instead. But I couldn't help any of it, that was sure, since I seemed to be snapping-to about one or two months late. I was a reader turning pages written some time ago, discovering what happened next.

We Take Communion

🜚 / About 3 a.m., Habits and Methods time Sunday morning, I realized that actually I did not know if they—Taurus and my mother—had called it quits or not. Maybe the same naïveté which first had me ignore the alien whiskey and the comforting extra weight in the house at night would now have me believe that, because negotiations for nuptial resurrection seemed to be under way, they (she and Taurus) would cease paramarital twinings. Hell, there was still the old man drinking a Bloody Mary with Mike's mother, one leg over the other, bouncing his Florsheim above the coffee table, and me and Mike outside checking out all right as prospective stepbrothers. And maybe they'd put on that conversation about remaining "friends"—even I knew that ruse. It's a diplomatic stunt. Bound allies suffer a falling-out and become political friends. Then they won't fight for each other anymore, but the treaties get a lot more delicate and worrisome, and somehow their close ties are more important

than when there were good military commitments
between them. But maybe they faked it—never had
the falling-out.

Anyway, I figured who was I kidding about them
—my ersatz Big Brother, whose one certifiable ID
card was scaring Theenie eighty-five miles in two
hours, and my pedagogic, sot mother, who was, I
have to admit, sharp for all that. What business was
it of mine anyway, and how was it better if they had
quit? It was precisely the stuff Taurus had taught me
to keep an eye out for, to know by indifferent acute
attention. So I would.

I had been all excited when I figured it out, throw-
ing that screen in the dirt and breathing hard. But
for what? What was the trouble, exactly? That *she*
did it? That he did it? That it was done to me? No,
I don't think so.

I think it was like at the Grand. There are some
dudes there who come out of the woods and woodwork with razor scars down their faces, across foreheads, through ears cloven into baby fists, from the
corners of eyes like scalding tear tracks. Even Jake
has a little one—it dents his nostril. And my information, which I got from watching the bug-
tussles they get in before Jake halts them with the
shortest shotgun in the world, is that two out of a
hundred of those scars had to do with gambling and
the remaining ninety-eight faces cut deep to bone,
blood flying like hogs stuck, are about *pussy*. And
even the two gambling fights are about not the
money lost but the pride lost in losing. And that's
close to the ninety-eight reasons for the other.

So pussy is the big nightclub reaper. It beats liquor, dancing, music, hemp, pills, rapping, racing cars, money, friends, and good times. And that's why, even at my youthful point of promise, my hair not even cropped in yet, I vibrate on the edge of the deep end over some bottle of liquor in a sack in a cabinet. What the hell can that stuff *be*, for God's sake? More than your finger inside your cheek, you rest assured. But what? I even think now, given this new disturbance I have had, that I am not going to know what it is even if old Altalondine dropped trou and said, "Get some of this cooter, stud, and if you can't kiss me you can pull my hair," and I, say, did—jumped on it like a woodpecker alighting on a sapling and did what you do—if this happened tomorrow, I would have no better idea why finding Taurus in Penelope's bower was so big a deal, and why you will cut somebody's nose off when under different circumstances it's enough to punch it in.

Well, I'm in these ugly meditations when the Doctor gets up and announces we're going to *church*. We do that about twice a year; once if it rains on Easter. I'm 3 a.m. fugued out anyway, so I sport up and we head out.

It's the usual. We go to Savannah, the closest place you can find an Episcopal layout. Right down in the slums, people already holding tallboys and blinking at the rising glare, we hit this pocket of new cars and a cathedral. All the dirt and smoke butts and dead banana trees changes to the soft, stained panes of biblical wonderment; and fresh acolytes with red-

and-white robes and white faces and red lips carry
gold candles; and the priest puts on twenty sashes
and linen underthings and gold-braid overthings
until he sweeps when he walks; and gold emerald-
studded pikes get carried around, with three prongs
for the Trinity; and the people kneel and stand and
sing and kneel and pray on red velvet cushions that
swing down for your knees like footrests under Grey-
hound bus seats, but of the finest, heaviest, wood-
pegged oak, not bent pot metal; and the sermon
intones with catch phrases like "more and more";
and the creeds, Apostle's and somebody's, get done;
and then we pray, and then we line up for Com-
munion. The Father wipes the silver chalice with a
beautiful linen rag large as a small tablecloth, turns
the cup two inches each time to keep you from having to drink where the last worshipper lipped it, as
if that takes care of the germs. But I don't care, I
always reach out very piously—that's to say, in slow
motion, the way you move for some reason to take
and eat the body of Our Savior—reach out and lay
my hand over the Father's in somber reverence to
the moment and then press down as the silver rim
clears my upper lip and suck a slug of wine that
should have fed six communers. I have to, because
the bread of His body is stuck to the roof of my
mouth like a rubber tire patch, and if I can't wash it
loose by swishing His blood around, I'm going to
have to dig it off with a finger, in slow motion, and
possibly gag.

When the service is over we go to a Howard
Johnson's for the business at hand. She wants to

talk. I should have known. She orders a grilled
cheese and takes one bite, as usual. She never eats.
It's the liquor. I get this ice-cream thing that looks
like Mt. Pisgah. She has cup after cup of coffee,
lights a cigarette.

"Well. I want to tell you something very important."

"Shoot." I don't like to be flip, but something about
parents draws that out.

"Your father and I"—she takes a long drag—
"have decided to get back together." She taps out
that new cigarette and lights another.

"Okay," I say.

"Contain yourself." I do, by destroying one of
Pisgah's promontories. "I thought you might be
excited by the news."

"The news is fine. But what's going to happen?"

"Well, a lot." Tap-out. Waitress, more coffee. "We
will move to Hilton Head."

"Oh, God. Have the Arabs got him?"

"Stop being a smart ass. He has a wonderful op-
portunity to join a good firm. And he is. We will
move there. You will go to Cooper Boyd."

"What about the house?"

"We don't know. We may sell it if it works out.
Or keep it for vacations."

"What about . . . Theenie?"

"She'll come to Hilton Head."

I'd heard enough. The good old days were on
a respirator. A boarding school and landed gentry snot-nose college-prep buggers for Simons
Manigault.

"I don't know how to put this," she said, "but in the past what became of you was more or less my bailiwick. That's shifted in the deal."

"Baseball."

She laughed. "I don't think that bad. But you will go to a good school, as your father wants. And what you read is up to you and them. You're a bright boy, son. Maybe I overdid things. Forgive me if I did."

"No, you did all right." You couldn't blame her for hedging the progeny gamble. I only held the shrink trip at three against her.

"No hard feelings?"

"Naaah."

"Give me a hug, then." She stood up right there and I had to follow suit and we hugged. I did like her. She was what they call a good soldier.

We sat back down and I glared at all the people looking at us and she smiled through more blue smoke.

This was heavy news. Taurus was good as gone. That didn't really bother me, especially because of the yet confusing whiskey revelation, but I knew I'd get over that and like him the same for showing me all he did, in the end. But I hadn't figured leaving the neighborhood—accessible mullet and the Baby Grand, the sporting life, being the Duchess's boy, and all that. That would be tough. I just figured I'd be tough, something was finally happening good or bad for damn sure, and if the good old days were on a respirator, I'd do them the service of going around and pulling the plug.

"All set?" she said, collecting her purse and keys.

We left Savannah and cruised north through the curiously hot, still quality of late Sunday mornings when your church clothes need to be taken off.

Taking Leave

�﹡ / Monday night I went up to Jake's expecting to engineer a big he's-a-good-fellow send-off, to collect a few condolences about leaving, etc. Yet I get there and stool up and order and swing around a couple of times making the joint blur, making the pool-table green send rocket trails of ball colors into the players. I don't feel bad a bit. More like *snappy*, I somehow feel.

They don't want me in there claiming hardship, carrying my howitzer can around for them to drop a tearful memento in and us to embrace like Boy leaving the jungle for Civilization and stiff British lips. All that's about as uncouth if not unethical as I could get. I'm supposed to be one of *them*. They'll know as soon as the first stick of furniture walks into that van what happened to me, it don't need no news conference.

Jinx comes up. His eyes are brilliant. We knuckle bump. He looks off for Jake and says to me, looking away for Jake, "Where you been?"

"I been around."

"Man, ain' seen you in a *long* time."

I shrug. "Just happens."

"Look so."

He got a beer and drank some of it. Nothing came to us to say. Then he says, "So take *care* yourself, man."

"You too, Jinx." He walks off. I notice he's dressed up. He dresses funny for a country Negro in the Grand. He wears cardigan sweaters and nice dark slacks—pushes up the sweater sleeves over his forearms—with matching socks or sometimes no socks. He looks like a college golfer. He goes over to the jukebox and studies it.

Jake's down at the other end, occupied with himself. He's got one foot up on a beer box, leaning on his knee, smoking, looking off at the wall. It's a slow night.

"Jake, what's the weather sposed to do?" I say.

"Might be sposed to rain."

We figure on that a bit. I had heard a rumble. Then he says, "You ready?"

"Nah," I tell him, setting my can back down in circles of water. "Not yet." He keeps smoking, looking at the wall.

I slip out.

Outside, it's thunder and purple dusk. I hustle. A black pickup about forty years old with hog-slop buckets in the back stops. An old guy squints at me. He's sixty to a hundred. No teeth. Gumming something. I get in. He nods. I did the right thing. We drive, a little slower than I was running, to the

Cabana road, where he lets me out. I wonder about the hog business—if he gets the slop free from restaurants, etc.—but don't ask him anything.

The palmettos sound like a stampede, crackling and brushing and popping. They're bristling around like fur, in waves and counterwaves. Jake sent me out the back door once at the Grand. I was all set to go out the front when his girl said, "Jake! You gone let that chile go out there?"

"Why not?" Jake said.

"It ain't nothing but a bunch of rowdy niggers out there. You, come on the back."

I went with her. I saw Jake call his momma to chain the dog. I went by the worms and a trail that let out down the road. I remembered all this walking in the whipping dark. The Cabana was lit up like a chandelier, crystal prism wobbling in the wind.

At the shack Taurus was snifting Old Setter with the window open on the beach side, watching the ghostly waves chomp. When it's dark you hear everything but only see a white roughness at the water's edge and sometimes a glassy curl out farther, enough to place the wave for you and let you count toward its break. Once like this I saw a shark tearing light out of the water, blasting loads of mullet in phosphorous fires in all directions, like the shark was a bomb and the mullet hot shrapnel.

But that night it was simpler. We just whiled it away. I should have known from the tone it was the end of us, like they say on a soap opera. Taurus asked me out of the blue, across the white enamel table and over our two amber oyster-jar snifters,

which we held like cups of mission soup, what were
Georgia and Alabama and Louisiana like.

I said Georgia was convicts and palmetto, but my
uncle built a lot of roads in the obscure parts, which
they said were good roads still, old-concrete-slab-
type roads with weeds in the expansion joints and
not all this asphalt-lobby shit on them. I said Alabama was a place the Doctor said the air was different, but it sounded like the famous Bear Bryant had
one half and the famous George Wallace the other
and you took your choice. I'd also heard there were
large shellcracker in Birmingham, somehow, but
who could say if they were the coach's or the governor's? But Louisiana I said was It. I heard an old
Mississippi lady tell of it once as "rich, old Louisiana." She said, "There's a lot of money in that state.
She's very rich." And she wasn't talking about new
money, or old money, or even money itself, but
some other richness about a place that is not necessarily all tied up in the bank. And then I told him
how the books seemed to bear this out. You had the
Kingfish book with that bodacious beginning, all
dug up right there at Baton Rouge—it must be the
place, if there's one left.

"Why do you ask?" I said after a while.

"Why not?"

We thought this one over.

"Well . . ." I said, highly articulate.

"Well, yes," he said. He looked around the room
and back at his jar of liquor.

He meant Theenie was coming back, which meant
Order, Restoration, including in its ramifications the

Progenitor's reclamation of the Barony and Penelope, and my riding a school bus regularly, and he meant swept floors at the house again, an end to custody junkets, an end to surrogate daddies, a beginning of baseball. I guess he hadn't heard we would go to Hilton Head.

"I'm thirteen years old in eight months," I told him. He nodded.

"Little League already has *stars*," I said.

"Flashes in the pan," he said. I guess I had told him before about my baseball training, before Daddy left. The Doctor takes me to a child psychiatrist at three to see why I can't read, and when we get home, Daddy puts me between third and second to see why I can't stop grounders. I failed the first test because I saw a relationship between an envelope and a cantaloupe and I failed the second because I saw a relationship between a crisply peppered grounder and a smashed face.

"Baseball," I said. "I see too much."

"It'll come in handy."

I think he meant the girl stuff. Even I knew that Diane Parker wasn't going to have much truck with worms and weenie-arms.

I wasn't really all that reserved about it, about grounders and girls and the end of coroners. That would put an end to listening to snout-first intrusions by the Doctor's suitors, to the suitors themselves, to the requisite Boy Act to get rid of them, and I could hear the sweet groaning rocks of the nuptial bower restored, and Theenie would be back and we could have talks, and she could do linen and run the vacuum and worry about the gubmen and make more pound cakes, and maybe get over her fear.

"Do you think she's your grandmother?" I said.

He had his liquor swirling in the jar on the table with some sand under it making a grinding noise. "I hope so," he said, grinning.

"You *hope* so?"

"Sure," he said. "What about you?"

What *about* me? I thought.

"Yeah, me too," I said, not at all sure what I meant, but the answer was faster than motive, and it was honest, only I didn't know what I meant. We looked out the window we had cut in the wall of common sense. We did not see any sharks tearing electric mullet from the Atlantic, only ghosts of waves making large noise. He was going to leave. He would drive back up the hard road through those odd inland pockets of salt-smelling air, and the fiddlers would come out and wave their ivory swords and then duck quickly back into their mysterious holes.

A Farewell to a Shack

❧ / The next morning I found the ground moon-pocked by the night's hard rain. Fiddlers were punchy, running dizzy. I got the mullet poles and took them to Theenie's shack, even though I knew he'd be gone. I took them to fend off the future. From the beach I could see the green shutters were up and tight. The rain had made the air very cool and the sand squeak. Only my face felt greasy in this new world.

He was gone. A note said, *Louisiana. Took your advice. Present under bed.* I found an old wooden stereo-viewer with a mahogany viewing hood and square glass lenses and a little wire rack on a sliding bridge for the cards, which you move like a trombone to focus. There was one card and I put it in. It was almost a headache while I slid the thing back and forth, then it was two separate pictures, each the same, of chickens in the air, and then suddenly they fell together and the scene was forty feet deep and the chickens were glorious multi-colored cocks with brass spurs. These wild spectators were watching them, their eyes all the colors of the cocks' feathers. I took the card out and looked at it. It was separate and simple again. It was something.

I put the viewer in a box of Theenie's things, what I guessed were her dearest things—a tobacco-colored Jesus on a felt base, and some funny little scarf things she folded up and left all over the place, and *Reader's Digest*s with religious bookmarks in them. I had packed all that up right after she left.

They were things would help her move in at Hilton Head. Not that she'd need much in the way of seed to take roots, because wherever we wound up in Hilton Head would be strictly uptown for her. She liked progress. A shack like hers was quaint only to people like me. To her it was acceptable *for its time*, and then it was something forever in the past, just like the W.P.A. was a neat time only for people who never saw the Depression.

She gave me a lecture on brooms and vacuum cleaners once. She had a house full of hardwood floors to do, to sweep, and she would not use a broom, which was efficient over a vacuum designed for carpet.

"I sweep *enough*," she'd say. "All my life."

"But Theenie, it's faster with a broo—"

"What *choo* know? *I'm* the one does it."

So she'd plug up this Kirby made of chrome and this most wonderfully supple, flesh-like rubber— must have cost about a thousand dollars, and *we* didn't buy it. It showed up the day she came.

"Simons, you Simons?" she said, the first words she ever said to me. "If you was a good boy to your

Theenie, you go up the road to the bush by the gate and get my valcum."

It spaced me out. "Do what?" To my theeny?

"Here." She handed me a piece of cloth. "There's a piece of this on the bush. Hurry up."

That was our introduction. I was already six years old. But she takes credit for raising me, all the same. And I found the Kirby stashed in the bushes by the hard road.

But back to the lecture. She'd plug up the Cadillac dirt sucker and I'd say, "Where'd you get that thing, anyway?"

"I got it."

"How?"

"I got it, ain't I?" A mock shriek.

"Yeah, but how?"

"You never mind."

"Why?"

"It's a secret."

"A secret?"

"A *secret*."

"What kind of secret?"

"A *milintary* secret," she'd scream. "Now git on, I got work to do."

And she'd run that thing for two hours, when you could have swept the house in ten minutes.

Well, it was like that, or would be, in Hilton Head. And she'd love it, as long as she got a fair shake on her room, if it wasn't smaller or too much bigger than anyone else's. She might have even forgotten the precious things I had in the box. Well, I toted it anyway, took it to the Cabana to be the first thing to go in that van.

Edisto Was Over

❦ / That van never came. We split. Left it all in place, like a museum. They were either serious about coming back for vacations, or they were real unsure about it working out, because not one drop of liquor left with us, or book, or toaster, curtain, camera, anything. Just some clothes.

I found myself standing on the porch by the wringer waiting for the Doctor, hand on the tub rim as I'd seen Taurus that first night he came to the house. I listened to it, too, a big conch shell of enameled sounds. The old rubber rollers were yellow and hard and wrinkled like skin. I tried to push the washer into the kitchen but it got stuck. I couldn't pull it out or push it through, and I could hear the Doctor rustling and knew she'd get mad, so one big shoulder-to and the rig squeezed in finally, lurching away on its caster wheels into the cabinets.

The Doctor gave it a queer look as she came through, and me one too, so I went over and settled the thing in a corner, patted it a little, like I was in control, and we locked up and left.

My mother and I rumbled by Jake's in the Cadillac in the hot middle of the morning—the lot a damp gray plot of crushed cans and shells and the Baby Grand a crummy dive-looking joint you'd never go in if you didn't know.

We wound up the road from shack to shack, blasts of close sound coming from the woods in between, then whining open spaces where we passed the bare yards. The salt smells of the ocean thinning and falling off, too. We got into some big oaks finally and then I started seeing pruned trees. Yards with grass in them. Heavy post fences. Private drives. A Mercedes. Negro on a mowing machine cut a swath about eight feet wide. Hilton Head.

As soon as we got there, I was handed over to Daddy like a baton in a relay. The next day he hurried me up to the eminent Cooper Boyd Academy for registration, which means they make sure your name can be found on certain genealogical pathways and you have the money.

I aced a little test they gave me and there was talk of my skipping a grade or two. "What academy is this young man transferring from?" the head dude asks Daddy. He says: "Put him in the grade befits his age." That had an effect. No more gab.

Daddy took me outside and said he'd be back, was going into town on "new business." I caught that odd modifier and noticed *he* was new. His suit was without wrinkles. Even his skin looked smoother. My idea of him all along was one of these modern store mannequins with stark wood-cut faces always too darkly stained and expressing some dire problem despite the perfect poise with which they model a

new suit—he had been like that during the custody
junkets. But now he looked more refined and natty,
a genuine relaxed Brooks Brother.

They took me to classes. One was a Latin class. I
never had that before. Was very interesting. There
was a photograph of Edith Hamilton herself on the
wall, inscribed to the teacher, a heavy woman carrying on like some folk were cruising for a caning if
they didn't shape up.

I said okay, I'll take that class, like I had a choice,
and they took me to geometry, where I knew what
acute and obtuse were but not their corresponding
meanings in that room, so I said that was fine too,
sign me up. I had the picture. I was an anomaly in a
regular soup of high-water khaki duck-asses, white-
soled Top-Sidered gentry bound for college and
careers suitable to family name, which is a hint
odd if you remember ten days ago I was an anomaly
in a backwater of blacks with the same family
names, bound nowhere, but bound.

Daddy retrieved me and we whistled on back to
the architect-conceived, Arab-financed, model rail-
roader's plot of paradise. I have this speechless
nervous reaction when we pop out of the untended
sticks of the scrub into suddenly pruned oaks, yellow
flesh wounds where limbs were sawn, their moss
all shorn. And miles become kilometers, shacks
condominia, marsh marina, and I feel like one of
those bullet-shaped birds in Audubon's drawer.

Doctor, Duchess, Soldier, Mother

❦ / When I say she's a good soldier I mean having a mother who's ordinarily regarded as a Duchess or a Doctor by everyone you know, but who's all right.

The day I took the bulldog by the ears was the first day I heard her called Duchess. I have found at the Grand that you can manage to hear Negroes say stuff under their breath in ways that sound like these whispery devil noises in exorcist movies. She was getting the bootlegged liquor for the party I had jeopardized by dropping the real liquor that time, and she was getting such a load that the early Grand drinkers came up to watch. She turned from Jake to, I think, Preston (I hadn't met anyone then) and told him to load it, which he did, even though he didn't work there. "Mr. Manigault will pay you for this Monday," she told Jake, and walked out. As far as I know, it was the only instance of credit at the Grand in history. And I would guess the liquor was over $200. Well, all around this scene you could hear on the edges of talk this whispered rodent-like sound, *the Duchess*. Jake looked surprised by her abrupt credit maneuver but not upset. I waited until she had cleared the front door and ran after her.

But I don't think that's when she was *named* Duchess. I put that earlier. It's another time I now know more about than when it happened. All I knew then was that Theenie was staying at the house at night late sometimes, and the Doctor and Progenitor would come in later. Now I know that only *one* of them would come in later. The other stayed gone. I also knew then that they were driving cars like Cale Yarborough on the last lap, you could hear them burning the hard road sometimes, and crushing palmettos on the way in. That, I now know, was just her. He'll do that ratchet noise with the transmission, and the six-inch skid, and that's all, while she'll paint a Darlington stripe from here to Savannah. Anyway, all this business was during the salad days of the breakup, I figure, and they were in a sleeping-out duel, and generally furious.

One thing that helps date all this is my teeth. I was having trouble collecting from the tooth fairy, and said something about it, and one morning a twenty-dollar bill showed up under my pillow. Probably the Progenitor was on home duty, came in, released Theenie, got in bed, remembered his parental fairy duties, couldn't find any change (couldn't find any teeth either, as far as I recall. They were in a jar because I had lost hope in the irregular fairy), and puts *twenty dollars* under my pillow. I believed all over again. And there was no effort made to recover the excessive grant, which you would rightly expect if they had been having regular home-style man-wife times, instead of the bust-up contest.

Anyway, one day during this time, I got off the bus at the hard road and just as I turned into our road one of the trees we have painted white to mark the curve *moved*. And smoked a cigarette. It was the Doctor, in white.

She had about twenty cigarettes crushed all around her, and was looking down the road. "I'll be in in a little while" is all she said. When I got home the phone was off the hook. I hung it up. And she came back in. Even today I don't know what all that meant.

But I do think that's when she became the Duchess. Some dude rounding the curve in a low deuce-and-a-quarter, thinking about nothing except getting up to the Grand, saw just what I did—a tree smoke a cigarette. Whoever it was figured out it was the white lady who bought the only beach house in this part of the world (which makes it a rich man's house), and somebody else said, "What she *doin'* out there?" "Yeah." "Standing out there." And somebody like Jinx would say, "Man, like a, like a *duchess* or something." And everybody would agree, *like a duchess or something*, no one the least bit curious to know what was like a duchess in it, and the name would fix. So that's the day. If it wasn't, it was merely another day, another eccentricity. "She drive that car like she a *duchess* or something." And she did.

Well, you can live with a Duchess easy, it's the Doctor part can get you. But she can be a good soldier right along. This good-soldier stuff shows up

all kinds of ways once you're ready to see it. Like the
formal sign-off in Howard Johnson's that day, when
she said it was all Jack London and baseball from
here on in. But do you know what? About three
weeks into my Cooper Boyd Latin tour, she casually
asked to see the *Commentaries*, which the class was
doing, *Gallia est omnis divisa*, etc.

I gave it to her and she tossed through it for about
half a drink and then put it back with my other
schoolbooks in their neat stack. And the very next
day, in that same stack, under those *Commentaries*,
was Horace on the bees! Leather-bound, dusty, and
I *know* it's fifth-year Latin stuff. Well, I don't say
anything, and she doesn't either, because she's
bound by the code of the good soldier to keep her
word about Rogering out and turning me over to the
Dodgers.

Also, she *stole* it. How soldier can you get? Nothing new there, she's done that before, from this old
library at her college that has been replaced by a
modern one of glass and elevators and photomag-
netic krypton turnstiles. There are all these old books
that she says will be sold for a quarter in a basement
sale one day that she takes as she needs—now, not
wholesale, but *at need*, like Indians and buffalo,
which is strictly soldier. Anybody on the outside
wouldn't notice good soldiering in this, he would
just see a stage mother in overdrive shoplifting, etc.
For that matter, no one would see that she did me
a favor going to the Grand for a trunkload of un-
stamped liquor when she could have called Vergil
and had the authentic stuff delivered. She made the
contact for us (for me) at the Grand with that

planter's wife act. That's what got me in there later, with no questions, by myself. That's what—her soldiering all along—got Taurus for me. All through the liquor and leftovers and coroners and mendacity is this other string-pulling shadowy maneuvering of things, mostly for me. So don't get down on your mother if she's drunk a lot, demanding, promiscuous, imperious, or anything. Because you might be wrong, you might not see the good soldier marching all along down in the trenches, for you. And you might be an igno, after all.

One time I remember she raised up out of the dark trench and squeezed off a round right in the open. It was at the party where Margaret Pinckney told the joke, and Bill called Taurus a thesis, and Margaret said some people had regular hopes still, and the Doctor told Jim to shut up. Well, I left the next part out because of the assignment. But I'm in a clear censor mode now so I'll add it on. After Margaret said the girls still had regular hopes, I saw the Doctor do the most amazing thing.

She kissed Margaret Pinckney full on the lips, like a man, lipstick and everything. Well, Margaret started crying and hugging her like they were long-lost relatives, one of whom had been missing in action and given up for dead, which was not amaz- ing, not for Margaret, still holding her tumbler of bourbon plumb over the Doctor's shoulder and call- ing for Kleenex with her free hand. Bill of course turns beet-red and runs for the bathroom and comes back recomposed but trailing unbroken toilet paper because he forgot to break it off. "That'll do fine right there, Bill," the Doctor says, and there's a laugh all around, and the women separate, and immediately the regular party hum-drum cranks up again—a gentle, assuring din that says everything's fine. Except the Doctor has a hard, clear pair of eyes deliberately looking nowhere, which she does to conceal purpose. That's what got me, that look. And that smooching was a doozie. That, as they'd say in the Grand, was most definitely jam *up*.

And I know this, too—soldiering once got her a purple heart. Because once upon a time she was a regular polite heroine in the small-town world of young virgins, as described by the most famous playwright. She went to a small college and was engaged to a handsome dude with papers and everything was set. Here the playwright always turns the screws with something like the girl catching her dude in another man's arms. Well, our soldier doesn't catch the fiancé in bed with a man, he just comes out and announces it, and the wedding is off, of course, and the rest of the play proceeds. She doesn't blame herself for the next two acts because the gent shoots himself, or screw an entire army base, but she *does* set-to on the nearest law school. She doesn't get crazier, she gets *saner*, with a vengeance. Lawyers, she figures, can't be that duplicitous, at least not with their bound commitment to uphold the law and all these unnatural-act statutes staring them in the face, so it's a much safer bet, getting one of these guys. The other guy was a poet, whose job, by comparison, was to challenge laws like that, anyway. So she wised up. That's why I'm half Republican and in Cooper Boyd instead of altogether socialist and taking dancing or piano lessons. It's like an outcross in dogs or horses. If she'd got that first dude, it would have been severe ideological inbreeding, and I might be shy or vicious or something. This way, the way Vergil tells it anyway (he breeds bird dogs), I can be a "good athlete," which means not baseball but just a solid individual partaking of two separate strengths and not two compounded weaknesses, I hope.

I realize now I sort of trusted her as the commander all along, the man in charge, like at Parris Island, where they say that even though what they do to you and ask you to do looks bad, if not insane, you won't get hurt if you do what they tell you. If you trust the man in charge. And on top of that, you'll *thank* them for making you let sand fleas burrow a quarter inch into your hide and for breaking your nose if you scratch at one. So I sort of knew or trusted, in this way at least, the principle of the man in charge, and she was him, and I believe it did not hurt, and I'll do that thanking in the end.

Taurus in a Spot of Trouble

✿ / This one's true. The one about Theenie's lost grandbaby might have been put together, fiction-mode. But this one happened.

Right before we went to that photo parlor—in fact, we went in there to rest after the trouble— Taurus got in a fight with a bum. We were in a little restaurant by the bus station in Charleston. A jukebox was playing and this little girl had learned to kick it and make the needle skip back to the beginning. She replayed the song about five times and was giggling when the bum called her over to the counter by saying, "Tell me what's on your Santy Claus list." It wasn't *near* Christmas, but she went for it. Well, it worked. The song ended. She ran back over and kicked the box, but too late. She got mad and the bum drank his beer.

Taurus gives her a dime.

The bum says, "Why 'ont you mine your own *bizzness*, buddy?"

Taurus says, "Why 'ont you mine yern?"

"Shih. Your kind chaps my ass."

The song came back in, the little girl beaming. "Care to dance, mister?" Taurus said. I was scared, but it was worth it.

"What are you—a hippie?"

Taurus looked at me. He was solid as a Marine. "Yes, sir. I'm a pacifist. Don't believe in violence of any kind."

"You don't believe . . . 'at's what ruint Veetnam. You step outside, son. I'mone teach you something."

"I'd rather listen to this rock and roll, sir."

"You're a punk."

That did it. I saw Taurus change. His nose flared. He put money on the table and walked out. They had a side alley. He went in there. Taurus suggested I go back inside and dance with the girl or something but I wasn't budging. It didn't matter because before anything Mr. Psoriasis II came rolling down the alley at a tilt after Taurus.

Taurus handled him like a bull, I swear. He never moved his feet much and every time the bum charged, headfirst, Taurus just caught him in the chest with short little punches that more than anything kept the guy from falling down. The guy didn't stop, so Taurus opened his hand and slapped him very hard on the face.

The man stood back, amazed.

"Why don't you quit?" Taurus said.

The man was congested and green-looking, with pink-and-red splotches on his face. He charged and tripped and fell at Taurus's feet and skinned half his nose off, and it bled from the inside, too. Taurus put a five-dollar bill by his head and said this speech in the tightest voice I ever heard him use: "Take a taxi to the county clinic. You broke your fucking nose."

We left. We tried to walk it off, I think. Just before we went into that photo parlor, Taurus said, "The only doctor that bastard's going to is M.D. 20/20." He was cool, but that deal had his nerves out. He was taking deep breaths every few minutes. I had the idea he had been very correct in all that crap, but he still didn't like it one bit. One thing was sure: Psoriasis II had a brand-new idea about hippies.

I cannot imagine my father doing anything like this. He would talk too much or call the heat or something. Then explicate it. But you could imagine Taurus directing a holdup with his hand in a paper bag suggesting a gun. I saw Jake stop a fight like that with his hand in a blue velvet Crown Royal bag. Taurus could do it, too. I'm rambling off the page. I'll miss him, is all.

But it was little things like this that will stand out. Not the fight—of course that's special. I was scared. But how *smart* he was gets me. All this crap off Psoriasis II and he never really gets riled out of shape. Just handles the situation without more or less than it demands—like being named "Taurus" and (apparently) deciding it will do. And never telling me his real name. Now, here's where he leaves this world. Someone else would correct you. Someone else would threaten the bum with the police or kill him in the alley. Well, I hatched a theory about it.

You can explain some of it with the heroin-baby rumor. Say he did have a heroin birth and had half his time sense, like memory, blown out. Then he could *have* to accept someone naming him. But I doubt that story.

Going into the photo parlor, I caught the essence of it. It was that he did not know what his life held and so studied it very closely. And I was different: mine held all the plans the Doctor and Daddy would negotiate, a cross-hatching of professional ambitions. I was not going to get to be a two-cylinder syntax dude at the Grand. I was, I am—I have to admit, that because my life is cloyed by practical plans and attainable hopes—I am white. Best thing to do, I figure, is to get on with it. So I said let's go in that joint for commemorative photos, my heart really beating then. I had one of these white hearts that lub-dub this way: *then—next*; and Taurus had one of these that go *now—next*; and the guys at the Grand went *now—now*. And you can't change that with decisions to be cool. You can't get to that *now—now* without a congenital blessing or disease, whichever applies.

So we went in, as I said, and took those shots, and I looked, apropos of all this horseshit, like a grub, and Taurus like a dusky man in jail.

The Official Hiatus
of Simons Manigault Begins

🙟 / **W**ell, here I am in old brand-new Hilton Head, which I thought was the first solid Arab bastion and a pure squat of Hell, but now it seems a scalawag of our own sold it out. He went all down the coast doing it. Got to Cumberland Island and he met the old Carnegie Steel people, who stopped him, sold their whole joint cheap to the feds. Yankee steel people preserving the South, Arabs the new Yankees, scalawags persisting as usual, and the place is consequently as confused as during Reconstruction.

But it's somehow pleasant enough here. The oaks are all pruned like I said, so they look like perfect trees in cement zoo cages. Small creosoted timbers are driven into the ground, forming borders for everything—plants, people, golf carts, restaurant parking. Condominia are all over, roads deliberately curve everywhere when they could go straight, the tinkling postcard marina, lobbies, lounges, links, limousines.

All the Negroes are in green landscape clothes, or white service jackets, or Volvos with their kids in tennis togs. It's something. Already their shacks and the bus riding with them smoking dope and the Grand scenes are dimming into the remembered vividness of a private gallery in my mind. I have to be on guard about it, about it all becoming photographs in a drawer, like Daddy remembering Jake's daddy's joint as a class operation, but Jake's is just a juke joint. That's not right. There's something fake in that. And what I worry is, I'll go back and do the same thing, or never go back, which will have the same effect. I'll just watch the photographs yellow.

We never talked about it or anything, but Taurus had a plan about this. He'd never be so eager to frame and crop the past, because that poses the present—you have to pose it to photograph it. And that means you can't take the future in its full array of possibility, because you're fixing to have to compose it for the present snapshot. It's all square, very square. Nobody in the Grand would ever do that. Nobody could. What presumption. There's not enough of an image to work with, to crop. So they don't shoot up the present with instant past, with warm immediate memories of how great it was, because it *wasn't* great.

Except the new Negroes in the Volvos, I guess they will try, they have enough to compose with, and you can't blame them. But at the Grand I couldn't go around that night and say goodbye. I would be freezing that night by anticipating Hilton Head, with a put-on spirit of lament, which would be phony to them, an insult, for if they were so

lucky as to go, to get a Volvo run at things and dress
their kids in new clothes, they wouldn't be bitching
about it or even hanging around to talk about it. If
someone did, he would come in with all his cash and
buy the house for the night. And when he got there,
and if his life became as comfortable and wonderful
as the white lives already there, would he start
snapping up the present with instant past? It's like
when you watch TV sports with instant replays. You
don't even get caught up in the live play, because if
you miss something you just run back in and see the
great action you missed—the scenes already past
which make the game you never saw so memorable.
Hell, maybe there's nothing so wrong with that.
Maybe Jake and those guys deserve better times at
any cost. But I think they could make a mistake of
a large kind if they ever come to Hilton Head and
act white. I can't express it. But I know you can
spend an evening with Preston and Jinx, and you
can't spend one with Jim and Bill and the coroners.
That's a *fact.*

I think of Jake with his foot up on the beer box,
elbows crossed on his knee, in his apron, smoking,
looking off, calling his mother if something goes
the dog's way. He knows he has only a few pieces of
the puzzle it takes to put together a life leaving for
a place like Hilton Head. And Taurus *gone*—hell
he'd just about handed me back Penelope and
Ulysses like he sort of did by setting me up with
Londie, his girl's prim cousin, instead of the looser
model I wanted, which would have made it all
different for me. And now I am a good gentry tyke in
Cooper Boyd, headed shortly for St. Cecilia Society

balls with a million Altalondine Jenkinses instead of talking trash with true Diane Parkers in roadhouses. He knew what he was doing. But the point is, he just cut out, didn't hang around for a photo session to preserve anything.

He'll walk into a Cajun bar down in Louisiana and be on the inside in two minutes with some trick of astute casual attention like calling that *Slitz* a little *Joe*, some new profession, name maybe, no regrets, no losses, no cumbersome ideas of what he is or is to be, no freight train of future bearing down on him, no comet of good old days burning him to a cinder of constantly failing memory.

When Taurus was gone I had a dream. You know how sometimes you think you've dreamed something before, or part of something before? And you dream again to develop it? I had that feeling. It was one of those dreams where nobody looks like anyone you know but they *are* people you know. And nothing follows or fits, but it all means stuff anyway.

It opens on a prison visitation room with a wire screen. An Elizabeth Taylorish woman, made up with red red lips and purple cheeks, plays the Doctor, and a Paul Newmany dude plays Taurus. He comes in under guard. Her eyes are rheumy, old rubbed-on peepers from a crying jag. "Take another cell, just for the night," she says.

"For God's sake," he says.

"He's a *man's* man. I have warned you."

"Be sure about dis ding, baby," he says, gangster-style.

Sniffling, tear-racked, she ekes out: "Chemistry never changes." She pouts like a minnow.

He rips up his side of the room. Guard doesn't even stop him. Just comes in and says, "Okay, buddy, it ain't the end of the world."

Then I think I dreamed of the morning after the night I learned that chemistry never changes, when I found Taurus making coffee at the Boy Scout camp, life on the open range. My sense is all messed up on it, when these dreams were. In fact, how much of the groaning rocks and chemistry talk was a dream, how much might have been the same thing as thinking I felt the comfort of Taurus coming in the house without knowing I knew it, I don't know. I do know when I got up I felt as dumbly wise as a fiddler crab. I looked at my mother and father very closely. They were jake.

So that's me. This is my motto. Never to forget that, dull as things get, old as it is, something is happening, happening all the time, and to watch it.

Living in a joint where the oaks are robbed of their moss and amputated of their little limbs *is* like living in an architect's model, and sleeping in redwood boxes *is* fakey, like being a cigar, and we now have furniture that *will not* make noise, and all those sailboats tinkling halyards against masts day and night, never been out of the harbor, *is* evil, or something, at least screwball as hell, but now I wonder: Who's to say all that stuff I left—the Grand, Taurus, the Georgia-Pacific pagoda and plantation of weeds—what if all *that's* the museum?

I got to heave to, hard-to-lee, or I'll get in the same trap I was in. Just because this place looks like a layout on a ping-pong table don't mean it ain't happening right here too. Whatever's happening. Hell, Taurus would become a bartender and watch the tennis ladies and seduce a share of them. And Theenie hauls in here, finds the vacuum, falls to in a minute. And the Doctor and the Progenitor get married and my custody junkets are over. It's the modern world. I have to accept it. I'm a pioneer.

Still, I haven't seen any mullet or mullet people. It's swordfish steaks from Boston now. That's where we're at, now. And the Hilton Lounge, cocktails, and red carpet, and I'm done with the Baby Grand. Even if Jake's still smoking while he studies the wall.

I'm done with the Baby Grand.

I'm done with the Baby Grand.

There.

I will say one thing: I've had some luck. There's not a baseball diamond on the island. I take a tennis lesson on Tuesday, a golf lesson on Thursday, and my new bar is a joint called the 19th Hole. I chat regular with the pro golfer, a real PGA dude. They serve me lemonade. The lessons, the fees, club sandwiches, everything goes on little register tabs I sign and Daddy picks up. We will be in father-son tournaments before long. "You never heard of Sam Snead?" the golf pro says, already looking around to tell somebody I haven't.

"This young fella never heard of Slammin' Sammy Snead," he tells them, and I'm a curiosity all over again. Then they tell me about the beautiful, glorious, gone past of golfing greats who were not kids off scholarship college golf teams but gentlemen who honed themselves on the grindstone of caddying for two bits a round. You never see these guys fold their arms and smoke and look for hours at a wall, knowing they don't know the whole alphabet of success, have all the pieces. They know the whole alphabet of worldly maneuver.

And how, I have to find out, did they ever come to think they know that?